D1234101

REVENGE

in the
Rockies

AN ALEX PAIGE MYSTERY

THERESA L CARTER

Contents

Chapter 1

Alex waited patiently, her hand curled around the handle of her suitcase. She looked around the lobby and her eyes fixated on a bronze sculpture of a horse bucking a cowboy. "Is that..." she wondered out loud, even though she was by herself.

"It's not real," a voice said, startling her.

She turned to see a squat woman standing beside her and had to rear back so she wouldn't accidentally kiss her. "It sure looks like a Remington," Alex said. "And hello, Harriet. It's good to see you."

Harriet swiped her limp hair behind her ear and gave Alex a small smile. "I'm surprised you're here, after what happened last month."

"If she stays home, the terrorists win." A man wearing a shirt plastered in parrots swooped in and kissed Alex on the cheek, then turned to face the other woman. "Hello, Harriet."

"William," Harriet sneered. The two reporters were not exactly fans of each other. "As I was saying, that sculpture is not a Remington. It's a fake, just like most of the artwork here," she said, with a sweeping gesture.

Alex's eyes followed her arm. Gilded-framed paintings depicting the old west adorned nearly every wall. A fire crackled in the center of the room, enhancing the luxurious atmosphere. Deep red wingback chairs flanked marble tables, and on top, more roses than seemed possible filled statuesque vases. She walked to the closest one, leaving her bag on the floor to hold her place in line, and gently rubbed a petal between her index finger and her thumb. While her nerves were still slightly numb from her cancer treatment, she could feel the texture. Not only did the roses look like velvet, they felt like it, too, but this was the velvet of mother nature.

"Fake or not, this room is gorgeous," Alex said. The man standing in front of her bag moved up to the reception desk, and she returned to the line, rolling her suitcase forward. "This place is right up your alley, Harriet."

Harriet grinned, a rare occurrence. "Yes, it certainly is. This is one of the most luxurious hotels and resorts in the country. My editor leapt at the opportunity when I told him I was invited. Why are you here, William? This seems a bit out of your—"

"League?" he responded snidely.

"I was going to say wheelhouse, but sure, whatever you want to call it."

Alex rolled her eyes. "Alright, you two. We are not going to start this already, are we?" William had the grace to look sheepish, if not a little defiant. "To answer your question," Alex continued, "I'm here because I sat in my condo for a year, and it wasn't by choice. I'm not about to hide away, not now when I'm perfectly able to get out. Besides, my best friend's competing. I'd be here whether they'd invited me to cover it or not."

"I thought William was your best friend?" Harriet asked.

"I have multiple best friends," Alex replied, exasperated.

"But you can't have more than one best friend. That's not what 'best' means."

The man at the registration desk walked away and Alex took his place, grateful for the interruption. She and Harriet had a contentious relationship that had only recently begun to smooth out. The last time the three journalists had seen each other had been the previous month in Door County, Wisconsin. It had been Alex's first time out after completing treatment for breast cancer. As a travel writer, she'd expected a normal trip: lots of food, drink, and exploration, and then she'd write about it all. But then one of the key players was murdered, and Alex barely escaped with her life.

After that experience, she was trepidatious, but she beat cancer. She wasn't about to let a little worry keep her from doing her job.

Behind her, William explained to Harriet that you can't put a limit on friendship. "Friendship is not pie," he said.

"But the word best means best. It means the top. It means there's only one. You can't have more than one best," Harriet huffed. Huffing was Harriet's preferred means of communication.

Alex accepted the key from the receptionist and turned around. "Harriet, Emily is my best female friend. William is my best guy friend."

"Don't you mean gay friend?"

"But even if they were the same gender, I see no need to limit my affections or my definitions. They are the best for different reasons, and yes, they are both the best." Alex turned her attention to William. "I'll wait over there," she said, pointing to the closest wingback.

"Sounds good, *bestie*," he said, winking.

Alex settled into the chair and began scrolling through Instagram. She stopped when she came to a picture of Emily with three other people. They were at The Broadmoor, the resort where all the chefs and journalists were staying during the filming of the inaugural episode of a new travel and cooking show. Emily stood next to a short woman with bright white hair and steel-rimmed glasses; the older woman looked like a marketing guy's idea of a grandmother. On Emily's other side, a man sporting a sleeve tattoo on one arm and a band of leather bracelets on the other scowled at the camera. Next to him, a blond man wearing a polo and khakis stood a few inches away. The four posed on a curved bridge over a lagoon. Emily's bright fuchsia hair complemented the pale pink of the adobe-textured hotel and contrasted with the blue-black of the water. Emily, of course, wore a goofy expression. *That must be LuEllen, Sergio, and Paul,* Alex thought.

"Ready, Miss Fancy Pants?" William asked, shifting his backpack.

"What, this old thing?" Alex grinned, standing up to show off her outfit. She wore mint green linen pants and a collarless cream silk blouse with flared sleeves. A bright pink sash at her waist, worn in honor of Emily, added a pop of color, and she'd accented the look with a bold, chunky necklace and earrings that repeated the trio of hues. She slid her hands down her hips, relishing the feel of the fabric and the strength of her body underneath.

This was new for her. Alex had always gravitated towards black, convincing herself she needed to be nondescript in her role as an investigative reporter. Now things were different. Not only hadn't she been a hard hitting journalist for some time, she also hadn't been able to board a plane for over a year. She decided she was going to celebrate every return to normalcy she could, and that meant donning an outfit that too often sat in the far back reaches of her closet.

William fingered the cool silk of her blouse. "Gorgeous. But how in the world did you manage to keep from spilling your in-flight cocktail? If I wore anything cream-colored, I'd be wearing everything else, too. Why do you think I wear things like this?" he asked, indicating his highly patterned Hawaiian shirt.

"Right. You're the epitome of nattiness. I don't think you know how to spill things."

"And you are not, so how'd you do it?"

Alex leaned over and whispered dramatically. "I asked for extra bev naps and used them as a bib."

William cackled. "Oh, that's so you, my dear. So very you."

"See you tomorrow, Harriet," Alex called, then looped her arm through William's, noticing he only had a backpack. "Is that all you brought?"

"Bellhop. I drove out from South Dakota and they only do valet here. I tell you; they weren't quite sure what to make of Bessie."

Alex laughed. "I imagine they don't get too many campervans here. It is The Broadmoor, after all."

"Especially one as dirty as she is right now. The badlands and the Great Plains are mighty dusty, my friend."

"Alex Paige? William Blake?" A woman holding a clipboard called to them. "I'm Becca, the producer of *Dining + Destinations.* Glad to see you've arrived safely." She glanced past them and consulted her clipboard again. "That must be Harriet Raven. You three are the last to arrive. Did you get your itinerary?"

Alex nodded. "Yes, thank you. Looks like we've got a busy schedule."

"Not as busy as the chefs. You should have a little down time each afternoon. Ok, then. I'll see you right here tomorrow morning at 8am. Don't be late," she said brusquely, then walked off to meet Harriet.

"You'll have to fill me in," William said, as they walked through the lobby. "I drove straight here, so I haven't had a chance to check email yet. And oh, look! A bar! Shall we?" He swerved towards the lounge before Alex could say anything.

"I've got time for one," she said, consulting her watch. "I heard they have glorious bathtubs and I aim to take full advantage of mine while I'm here."

Since it was a Tuesday night, there was plenty of room at the U-shaped bar. A couple sat next to each other on one side, their foreheads nearly touching. Alex picked a corner seat on the other side and rolled her bag next to the railing at the base of the bar. William automatically sat around the corner so they could see each other while they talked, putting his backpack on the seat next to him. They browsed the cocktail menu and William selected a Gold Mine Martini while Alex ordered a Macallan 15, neat.

"Oooh. Going for the good stuff, I see."

"I'm dressed for it. Seemed like the thing to do." She dipped her fingers in her glass of water and sprinkled a few drops into her scotch, then took a sip. "Oh, that is so good."

"Ahem," William said, his glass poised in the air. Alex tapped her rocks glass to his coupe. "Cheers," they said.

"I still can't believe you've never met Emily," Alex said, after taking her second sip of the smooth liquor. "As many times as you've come to Chicago, and we couldn't make it happen."

"I was always working and my editors had other ideas. I kept pitching a dinner at *Elements*. I told them it's the perfect type of restaurant and my gorgeous photos would look really great in glossy."

"And you probably said it exactly like that," Alex said, shaking her head affectionately. "Well, after Emily wins this, your editors will be clamoring to include her in your next stories. In fact, they'll be kicking themselves for previously ignoring your wisdom."

"As they often do," William said, touching his glass to hers with a ting.

"You promised," the woman across from them shrieked, rearing back from her companion. "You bastard. You promised." The man laughed and said something too quietly for them to hear. The woman threw her drink in the man's face and stormed out. The bartender walked over to the man, handed him a glass of sparkling water and a white towel, placed a rocks glass filled to the rim in front of him, and walked away.

"Isn't that?" William whispered, although his whispers were always so loud they could be heard several feet away.

"Eric Dixon," the man said, wiping his face and shoulders. He threw the towel on the bar before taking a drink of what Alex presumed was a cocktail. "Good thing she drinks vodka and not red wine," he chuckled. He stood up and walked over to them, carrying his drink. "I'd shake your hand, but mine's a little sticky. Hey Max?" he called to the bartender. "Bring me more water and another towel." The man pushed aside the barstool with William's backpack, never taking his eyes off Alex. "She's gorgeous, isn't she."

William knew better than to respond. Alex met Dixon's eyes and held them, refusing to smile, blush, or have any reaction that would give this pompous man a modicum of satisfaction.

"You'd be prettier if you smiled. And grew your hair long."

Alex felt her hand lift, wanting to touch her hair, a nearly sub-conscious reaction. William reached under the bar and grabbed it. She knew it wasn't to prevent her, but to offer comfort.

"Max?" William called. The bartender looked up. "We'd like our check, please." Max placed the folio in front of William, who put his room key inside. Alex continued to stare at the man. Eric Dixon. The man who owned the company sponsoring the show Alex had flown to Colorado Springs to cover because her best friend was a competitor.

Dixon leered at her. "Going so soon? Stay awhile. Max, get their next round on me."

Max picked up the folio, arching his eyebrows. Alex stood up, slung her purse on her shoulder, and turned to the bartender. "Thank you for the scotch," she said, then wrapped her hand around her suitcase handle and walked out of the lounge, her head held high the entire time. She kept walking, her pace quickening as her heels clicked on the marble floor until she pushed through the glass doors to the outside. She gulped in the cool night air and turned her face to the moon, closing her eyes.

Alex heard the doors behind her open. William came to her side, took her hand, and the two silently crossed the curved bridge and lagoon she'd seen earlier in Emily's picture. They reached the elevators.

"427," William said. It was the only word he'd spoken.

"429," Alex responded. "Thank you."

"Always."

Chapter 2

Alex lowered herself into the warm water, resting her head against the back of the tub as the bubbles reformed on the surface. Taking a bath was a luxury she'd missed during her months of treatment. With her lumpectomy, the additional surgery to remove cancerous lymph nodes, chemotherapy, and radiation, baths had been prohibited. This wasn't her first soak since completing treatment three months earlier, but it still felt like a forbidden treat, which made it even more luxurious.

She sipped her glass of sparkling water, fresh from the springs that made this area of Colorado famous. *Decadent*, she thought, as she popped a profiterole in her mouth. *This is completely decadent.* Alex wondered how Emily was doing. It was odd to be so close and know she wouldn't be able to spend much time with her. At home in Chicago, the next-door neighbors saw each other daily, in and out of each other's condos like they were connected instead of separate apartments. It worked out especially well for Alex, since her best friend was one of the best chefs in the country. Emily had been farm-to-table before it was a "thing," working with local farmers and shopping for *Elements*, her Lincoln Park restaurant, at Green City Market. She constantly innovated, and when she was home, Alex received the benefits of her efforts.

In the past year, Alex had been home a lot. Swirling her arms in the bathwater, feeling the liquid slide over her body, Alex reflected on how different her life was now compared to the months of her treatment. She fully believed that Emily's unwavering support helped her get through the most difficult time of her life relatively unscathed. Well, except for the multiple scars, misshapen breast, and the skin discoloration and rash the radiation left behind. Internally, she was much healthier because of her friend. It didn't hurt that Emily would frequently ask Alex to do her a "favor" by taste-testing her culinary creations. Alex knew that was Emily's way of making sure she ate, and ate well.

Alex wasn't surprised that her friend was one of the final chefs selected for the show. She also knew the next four days would be increasingly difficult as the competition narrowed. While every chef would walk away with something, only one of them would get an entirely new kitchen. Alex didn't envy the judges and was glad all she had to do was eat and write about it.

She thought about the man from the bar. "*You'd be prettier*," she mimicked, then ate another profiterole. "What an unmitigated ass," she said, then laughed at herself. "Better watch this talking-to-yourself thing, or people are going to get worried."

Like William, once the man had faced them, Alex recognized who he was. Eric Dixon, the heir to Dixon Kitchens. His playboy lifestyle earned him more press than his eponymous company received, most of it unflattering. She figured that's why they were sponsoring the semi-reality show. She knew from Emily that Dixons were the top of the line, and priced to match, but they wouldn't be able to command those prices for long if Eric continued to damage their image.

Alex pulled the plug to let the water drain. She knew, for Emily's sake, she was going to have to try to keep her distance from Dixon. If she didn't, she didn't trust herself to stay calm the next time he said something rude. And she knew for a fact that he would definitely say something rude.

Alex and William entered the hallway at the same time. William looked at her with disgust. "You've been up for hours, haven't you?"

She grinned. "Yep. Haven't you?"

He groaned. "You know better than that."

"I don't get it," Alex said. "How someone as active as you are could hate mornings."

"I like the nightlife."

"You've got to boogie."

"On the disco rouuuuund, yeah." William sang while sliding into the elevator. "I peeked at the itinerary last night. Today, despite the early beginning, should be fun." The plan was to ride the cog railway to the summit of Pikes Peak. Then they'd interview some of the chefs before that evening's dinner at Dixon's showrooms.

They reached the lobby. Alex saw Emily, and the two friends skipped towards each other before hugging. "What's a hot chef like you doing in a place like this?"

"Waiting for a smokin' writer like you," Emily replied. "William!" She wrapped her arms around him, then pulled back. "I see what Alex means. You're hot in your pictures, but in real life? You are gorgeous."

"Oh, I like you," William said, then turned to Alex. "You can keep her."

"Nobody keeps this one, my friend," Alex said.

"Got that right. Let me introduce you to the other chefs." Emily led them over to a cluster of three standing near the bellhop station. Alex recognized them from Emily's Instagram photo. They barely had time to shake hands before Becca, the woman who'd been holding the clipboard the night before, cleared her throat, louder than Alex had heard anyone clear their throat before.

"Morning. Have we got everybody? Mike? Where's MJ?" she asked a man wearing a plaid flannel shirt and lugging a camera set into a giant gimbal. A short man holding bags and tripods followed closely behind him.

"No idea. Maybe you should ask Dixon." he answered.

"I'm here. I'm here. Don't get your panties in a wad," a skinny blonde wearing platform boots and a Canada Goose sleeveless vest growled. "Oh!" she stopped suddenly, realizing she had an audience. She smiled and her face lit up.

"Wait a minute," William hissed in Alex's ear.

"That's her," Alex whispered back. "That's the woman from the bar last night."

"Interesting."

"And about to get even more so," Alex said, pointing down the hall where Dixon was striding towards them.

Becca glared at the two new arrivals. "So glad you've decided to join us. Now. Everyone, this is MJ. She's our show's host. Lumberjack over here is Mike, our cameraman. His assistant is Dennis. I'm sure you all recognize Eric Dixon." Dixon smiled and gave everyone a thumbs up, then headed out the front doors, ignoring MJ, the woman who'd thrown a drink in his face the night before. Alex shivered. He gave her the heebie jeebies. "And I'm Becca. I trust you writers and chefs can introduce yourselves to each other," Becca continued.

"Here's how it's going to go. We're producing a show, and that means you need to be punctual. You also need to be accessible by phone at all times in case something changes. Chefs, Mike and Dennis are going to be your new best friend. Writers, make sure you stay in the background. You are not part of the show. You are here to observe and interview. Of course, you also get to explore with us and eat what I'm sure will be incredible food." Becca consulted her watch. "Time to go. It's a short drive to the station, so don't worry about who sits where, but I want all the chefs to sit together on the train." She turned on her heel and walked outside.

Alex, William, and Emily looked at each other and shrugged. They started to follow Becca outside, but MJ and Mike walked in front of them. Alex saw Mike give MJ questioning look. The host shook her head. "Later," MJ said, glancing back. Alex turned her head away.

Now, what was that all about? she wondered.

Chapter 3

T he train car lurched and Alex braced herself on William's knees.

"If you want to sit on my lap, just come on over," he said.

"Thanks, Santa, I'm fine. Besides, I'm probably on the naughty list."

"You? Pshaw. You may not be Miss Goody-Two-Shoes, but you'll always be on my nice list."

Harriet rolled her eyes. "Would you two get a room already?"

Alex and William looked at each other and burst out laughing. "Well, we could," he said, "but I don't think it would have the intended results."

"No, it certainly wouldn't," Alex agreed. "Harriet, you know better than that."

Harriet huffed. "Of course I do. I've spent enough time around you two. But could you please stop being so... you, and listen to the conductor? We are here to work, after all." Harriet looked down at her notepad and William mouthed to Alex *We are here to work*. Without looking up, Harriet elbowed William. "We are," she insisted. And huffed. She gripped her pen and notebook and stood up. "I see an open seat up there, so I'll leave you two to your — your shenanigans."

William watched Harriet negotiate her way through the narrow aisle to a spot three rows up. "Oh goodie. She got a window seat." He sounded like he was mocking Harriet, but Alex knew he was sincere. He turned back to face Alex. "I know she's only thirty-something, but I swear there's an old maid in there."

"I guess she's had it pretty rough," Alex said. "She told me a little last month. However, she does have a point. We should be listening because we are here to work, and besides, this railway is fascinating."

Through the overhead speakers, the conductor gave factoids about the history of the cog railway that climbed to the top of Pikes Peak. The producer of the show had reserved an entire car for the writers, chefs, judges, and film crew. Alex peered down the car, which was easy to do since she was facing backwards and they were on a steep incline, and waved to Emily.

"I wish I could go sit with Emily," Alex said.

"What, I'm not entertaining enough for you?"

"Goof. I want to see how she's doing, that's all."

"Quite a view, isn't it?" Eric Dixon stuck his head between her and William to look out the window. Alex ignored him, watching a cascading waterfall as the train inched uphill.

"It certainly is," William replied.

"You don't have anything like this back in Chicago, eh?" Dixon said. She could see with her peripheral vision he was looking at her. She turned her head to face him. That he knew where she was from made her even more uncomfortable. "What do you think so far?" Dixon continued, standing upright and then leaning on the back of the seat while still watching Alex.

"I love the concept," William answered. "Part travelog, part cooking competition, but no cutthroat B.S. and no screaming chefs. Well, not many screaming chefs. Just enough to keep it exciting, I'm sure," he said. "And we get to eat dinner in Garden of the Gods on Saturday? Amazing. How'd you pull that off?"

Dixon pointed at Becca, who sat across the narrow aisle from the four chefs tapping on her phone. "Becca gets all the credit for that. She's the organizational guru. Of course, dropping the Dixon name doesn't hurt. *Everyone needs a Dixon in the Kitchen,*"he chanted, mimicking the commercials. "Or in this case, in the Garden." Dixon laughed, clearly proud of his joke. "I'll let you get back to the view," he said, still fixated on Alex until he walked away. He moved up the car and she heard him launch into a similar conversation with Harriet.

Alex shuddered. "Ick," she said.

"Right?" William said. "That man is simply gross. I wouldn't trust him to walk my dog."

"You don't have a dog."

"But if I did, he wouldn't get ahold of that leash. No way. I'm surprised he gave Becca any credit."

"It makes sense to me. He seems like he'd be happy to let others know he doesn't have to worry about all the little things. You know she runs the show," Alex said, watching Becca as her thumbs flew over her phone's screen.

"Yeah, that's pretty obvious. Especially considering all the trouble Dixon's been in. Rumor is they want to kick him out of the company." William was talking to Alex, but he wasn't looking at her, and she knew he was watching Dixon.

"Didn't his father found the company?"

"Yep. And Junior's doing his darnedest to run it into the ground. My guess is they're sponsoring this show as a way to prove they're still the best," William explained.

"That's what I was thinking. No matter what the reason for the production, I know Emily would love to win that grand prize. A whole new kitchen? That would be life-changing for her, and her staff. Her current kitchen is holding on with duct tape and hope." Alex checked on Emily, who was looking out the window while Paul prattled on. Alex knew he was prattling because Emily kept rolling her eyes. "She hates taking this time away from *Elements*, but it could make all the difference."

Rocks the color of burnt sienna crayons covered the landscape as they climbed higher. Alex could now see over the trees. She listened as the conductor explained they were near Inspiration Point, the view that inspired Katharine Lee Bates to write *America, the Beautiful*. Dixon was a jerk, but he was right about one thing: there was nothing like this back home.

The train slowed to a stop. The conductor warned everyone to make sure they got back to their seats within forty minutes. "You know what we call people who miss the train?" the conductor asked. "Hikers."

The chefs filed out first and Emily waited for Alex and William to alight. Emily looked over her shoulder with alarm; Alex turned to see Harriet leaning against the car. "Hey there, you doing okay? You look a little pekid."

Harriet gulped and held up her index finger. Emily handed over her water bottle. "Here. Drink. It's got electrolytes." Harriet grabbed the bottle and gulped, then swiped a stray drop from her chin.

"Thank you."

"That altitude'll get you," Emily said.

They walked away from the train. Alex paused before they'd gone more than a few steps. "Harriet? Want to join us?" she asked.

"No. I'm fine. Go." She brushed them away and leaned against the train. Alex watched her for a moment, then shrugged and wrapped her arm through William's, leading him from the train towards the visitor center.

"It's the altitude, all right, but not in the way you think," William said to Emily. "I think our dear Ms. Harriet has an issue with heights."

Although the whole mountain top was fenced off so nobody could just fall over the side, Alex knew that rationale wouldn't assuage Harriet's fears. "All these years and I didn't know this about her," Alex said. "Think she'll be okay?"

"Harriet? She'll be fine. See? Becca's got her."

Alex turned to see the larger woman maneuver to Harriet's side so she blocked the drop-off. Satisfied, Alex continued up the path between William and Emily. The three entered the visitor center. Alex paused to admire the towering glass front that provided a panoramic view of the surrounding landscape before making a beeline for the interactive exhibits. Emily headed towards the cafe, explaining she wanted to see if she could discover their method for making doughnuts at such a high elevation. *Always the chef*, Alex thought, admiring her friend's dedication.

Alex herded William through the exhibits, quickly taking pictures of each one. She'd review them later. They had a very short time and she needed to use the bathroom and then see the view.

They walked outside and followed the trail to the elevation marker that proclaimed they'd reached the summit of Pikes Peak at 14,115 feet. Sergio and LuEllen were already there, posing with the marker and trying to take a selfie. Sergio's bare arms revealed his sleeve tattoo featuring Dali's melting clock. "How is he not freezing?" William asked. "Oh yeah—because he's hot. Hey you two," he called to the chefs. "Want me to take your picture?"

Sergio handed him his phone, and LuEllen reached into her knee-length parka to get hers and gave it to Alex. "Mine, too, y'all." With her white hair, round face, and steel-rimmed glasses perched on the end of her nose, she and the t-shirt clad Sergio made an incongruous pair, and Alex grinned at them as William framed the picture. "Say Pikes Peak!" she said.

The two smiled. Sergio's face transformed from what looked like a permanent scowl into something radiant. Alex heard William inhale. "Would you look at that? I mean, I knew he was gorgeous, but when he smiles? Makes my knees quiver, and it's not from the altitude," he said out of the side of his mouth.

Alex shook her head, something she did often around William, and took a picture with LuEllen's phone. "I thought you were ga-ga for Billy?" Billy was a detective they'd met the previous month who surprised everyone by falling for William. Alex still couldn't help giggling about the names.

"My darling Alex, how many times do we have to go over this? I appreciate beauty. Just because I'm enamored with a certain man of the police persuasion doesn't mean I can't appreciate this tattooed specimen."

Sergio and LuEllen thanked Alex and William for taking the photos, then LuEllen offered to take one of them. After they posed, Alex looked at the time. "Darn. We've only got twenty more minutes. I'll set an alarm. C'mon. Let's see as much as we can and get back to the train."

Chapter 4

Alex leaned over the railing, the crisp mountain air assaulting her face and leaching every single bit of moisture. Her eyes stung. She tried to wet her lips, but her tongue dragged like sandpaper. Her skin felt like a towel that hadn't been washed in far too long.

She grinned. This is the life, she thought.

Alex swept her gaze across the city below her and the plains beyond. "So this is what it's like to summit a fourteen-er, eh?"

William grinned back. "Yep. Although we took the easy way."

"How many have you climbed? Five? Six?"

"Seven, not including this one, because taking a train to the top definitely doesn't count."

Alex turned to see Harriet standing behind them. "Did you want to see this?"

"No, no, I'm okay," Harriet said, wisps of hair escaping from her knit cap.

Paul, wearing a puffer jacket and a trapper hat, grabbed Harriet's arm and began pulling her towards the railing. "You're not afraid of heights, are you?"

Harriet's face got even whiter. Alex could see the terror on her face. "Paul! Stop it," Alex commanded.

Paul's lips thinned, but he let Harriet go. She scooted back to safety, collapsing on a bench and putting her head between her knees. Alex rushed to her and began rubbing her back. Harriet calmed and straightened up, dismissing Alex's ministrations. "I'm fine. I'm fine. Really. Go back and look at your," she waved her hand towards the railing, "whatever."

"I had no idea," Paul said, his face now smoothed with a mask of concern. "I was trying to help. I thought you'd want to see it."

"Don't," Harriet said. "If I want your help, I'll ask for it." She pulled her cap down and walked away from the small group towards the bright red train perched on the side of the mountain, gripping the fence as she went.

Alex took one more glance at the scene below. She could see the red slabs of Garden of the Gods and marveled at the contrast of the ancient rocks jutting up in the middle of a city.

"It's so bizarre," William said.

"It's beautiful." Reverence filled Alex's voice. Even if Emily hadn't been a contestant, Alex would have accepted the invitation to cover this show. Garden of the Gods was a bucket list item, and within a few days she'd get a much closer look. The final dinner and the reveal would take place within the park itself.

Alex heard part of their group approaching and turned around, smiling when she saw the red, beaming cheeks of her neighbor and friend. "So Em, did you get their secret?"

"You better believe it," Emily said, looking distinctly pleased with herself. "I'll now be able to make doughnuts at 14,000 feet and above."

Behind Emily, Sergio shook his head, his permascowl back on display. "And she won't share."

"Why should I? Would you share with me?" When he cracked a small smile, she punched him lightly in the arm. "There you go. Maybe you'll just need to figure out how to be more charming."

Paul rolled his eyes and looked between Emily and Sergio. "I think he knows everything he needs to know about being charming."

Emily guffawed. "Oh no, he's definitely got a lot to learn."

William leaned towards Alex. "Looks like we've got a couple cocks fighting over a hen over here."

"Em is no hen, my friend. They'll end up picking their beaks off the ground if they even try."

LuEllen hurried towards them. "Time to go, time to go," she rushed, panting.

Alex looked at her watch and frowned. The timer she thought she'd set to make sure they wouldn't miss the train was still waiting for her to tap *Start*. William grabbed her hand. "C'mon," he said. "Last one to the train's a hiker!"

Alex and William ran towards the red car. Her foot slipped on a patch of ice. She gripped William's arm and Emily grabbed the other one. "Whoa there, Nelly. It's not like they'll leave without us."

"Oh yes, they will," Paul said. "Happens all the time."

"That's right," William said. "You're from here, aren't you?"

Paul nodded as they hurried. "Used to be. We moved to Malibu when I was a kid, but there's still family here," he panted.

"I've heard wonderful things about *Siren*," Alex said.

"Thanks. I had to shut down this week so I could be here," Paul said. "My staff appreciates the time off, though, so it's fine."

Sergio scoffed. "You shut down your restaurant? Don't you have a decent sous?"

Emily glared at Sergio. "Why are you so rude?" she asked. "I shut mine down, too. It's just easier since they wouldn't be able to get hold of me."

"You need a new sous," Sergio muttered.

"What did you tell them?" William asked. "You're under an NDA, right? So you couldn't tell them what you're really doing."

"Easy. I told them we'd take a week off to rest up before the holidays. I usually do it in October, so I just moved it up a couple of weeks," Emily replied, then walked down the sidewalk to board the train, followed by Mike and Dennis. The cameraman and his assistant had been hanging in the background, shadowing the chefs as they wandered around the summit.

Becca waited at the door and ushered Paul inside. LuEllen bustled in front of them, and Alex could hear her ragged breathing. "Sergio!" Becca called. "Get a move on!" Sergio ran down the sidewalk, then stopped directly in front of Becca and bowed. "Go on, you fool," Becca said, a smile taking the edge off, then motioned for Alex to get into the car. Alex entered, followed by William. They collapsed into their seats. William took a sip of water and urged Alex to do the same. He looked up with alarm. "Harriet? Drink some more water, dear. You look, and I mean this in the kindest way, positively dreadful."

Alex turned around. William was right. Harriet's already fair skin was bone-white and she was leaning her head against the window. Alex pulled an extra bottle of water out of her bag, opened it, and passed it to Harriet. "Drink this," she commanded. Harriet complied.

"Thank you," she rasped. The only color on the woman's face was her bright red nose. She pulled out a tissue from under the wristband of her coat and blew noisily. She tried handing the bottle back to Alex. "Keep it," Alex said. "I've got another one."

While Harriet drank, Alex glanced around the train. Besides the three of them, there was a small handful of journalists who'd been invited to cover the new show. Alex didn't know the other writers, but she'd read their work. Most of them covered aspects of travel, but a few focused heavily on food. It seemed like everyone was accounted for.

Almost everyone.

Harriet looked out the window. "What on earth is she doing?" she asked with scorn, and Alex knew she was feeling better.

Alex followed Harriet's gaze to see MJ standing on the sidewalk several yards from the train, talking and gesturing with both hands. Across the aisle, Becca tapped away on her phone. She looked up and saw MJ, then looked back down, shaking her head. Mike knelt on one of the benches and focused his camera out the window. The conductor stepped inside, the door snicked shut, and the car lurched. MJ's head shot up. She ran towards the car, tottering on her platform boots. The train moved slowly enough that MJ could follow along with it, beating on the door. "Let me in!" she shouted. "You have to let me in right now!"

The conductor looked MJ in the eyes, tapped her watch, and shook her head.

"Looks like we've got a hiker," William said.

Alex pulled her eyes from the still-yelling woman, who slowly diminished in size as the distance between her and the train increased. "That's not going to go over well."

"Of course it would be her," William said.

Alex nudged his knee. "Now, now. That's not very nice."

"Right. You don't even like her," he said. Alex raised her eyebrows. "Yes, it's that obvious."

"She reminds me of a certain blonde," Alex said.

William shuddered. "Oh, now she was a piece of work." They both still harbored a bit of PTSD from their experience in Wisconsin.

The conductor walked by. "Excuse me," Alex stopped her. "How often does someone get left behind?"

"Daily," she said, confirming what Paul had said earlier.

"How will she get back down?" William asked.

"She can either wait for the next train, which will be in four hours, or she can get someone to come pick her up. The road's open, at least." She continued walking down the aisle.

"Guess it's a good thing we took the early train," William said.

"I wonder if this will affect tonight's show," Alex said.

"No, it won't," Becca answered without looking up from her phone. "I've got someone up there to drive her down."

"Smart," William said.

"Not my first rodeo." Becca said.

"I take it you didn't tell her?" Alex asked.

Becca's lips curled in a serpentine sneer. "Now why would I want to encourage her bad behavior? Although I suppose I am by having a car waiting. But, as they say."

"The show must go on!" William finished.

Becca resumed her seat across from the chefs. "Mike," she called. The cameraman turned towards her. "You know you can't use that footage, right?"

He grinned sheepishly. "What, no blooper reel?" he asked, before flopping into the seat next to William and resting his video camera on his lap. "Of course, MJ would be the one to miss the train."

"That's what I just said," William replied. "See? It's not rude if it's true."

"That's not how it works," Alex said, then turned to Mike. "I take it MJ's a problem child?" she asked.

Mike rolled his eyes. "You have no idea. Wanna-be prima donna. Most hosts aren't like that, but she was Dixon's first—and only—choice, so we're stuck with her. At least she's good on camera."

"Have you worked with her long?" Alex asked.

"Nope. This is my first gig with Dixon, and it's her first show. Apparently she was his kids' nanny."

Chapter 5

William spit out the water he'd just sipped, then wiped a few stray drops off Alex's knee. "Seriously? She was his 'nanny'?" he asked, using air quotes around the title. "Wait—Dixon has offspring?"

"Hard to believe, isn't it?" Mike said. "Two boys. They live with their mom."

"Mom got the boys; dad got the nanny. Got it."

"Mom definitely got the better deal," Mike said. "Sorry. I shouldn't be saying all this. MJ just makes my job way more difficult than it needs to be."

"I can only imagine. Bet she wants to approve every shot before you send it out," William said.

Mike cocked a finger and pointed it at William. "You got it."

"Stop. It. Before I throw you two out the window," Emily said, loud enough for the entire car to hear. William craned his neck to see what was happening and Alex tilted her head to see around him. Mike had already gotten up and trained his camera on the chefs, who were obviously arguing. Becca squeezed by him and sat down next to Alex, propping her feet on the seat next to William.

"Ah, drama drama drama. I love the smell of drama in the morning," Becca said.

"Makes for better TV, eh?"

Becca flicked her gaze to William. "Yes," she answered him. "It sure does. This may not be your typical cutthroat competition, but we still want some tension."

"How much of that goes into which chefs make the final cut, so to speak?" Alex asked, genuinely curious.

The producer twisted her head toward Alex. "None whatsoever. The judges are entirely independent and we have no influence on who they choose. That's why they do blind tastings."

"But since this is really just a promotional vehicle for Dixon Kitchens," William asked, "does it really matter?"

"You're forthright. I'll give you that." Becca took a drink from her water bottle. The chefs had quieted down, mainly because Emily had forced Sergio to move to a different seat. Becca wiped a drop of water from the corner of her mouth and continued. "That's precisely why it needs to be even stricter than other shows. Our clients are the kinds of restaurateurs who can afford to spend $30,000 on one appliance. Our reputation is on the line. If it seems like we're playing favorites, well, that wouldn't look so good."

"Why not?" Alex asked. "From the pitch and itinerary, the show seems to be just as much about the destination as the cooking. I don't think people are going to be too scandalized by apparent favoritism, if you do have a favorite." Alex paused, then whispered dramatically. "And if you do, then it should totally be Emily."

Becca smiled. "That's right; you two are friends. To answer your question, the viewers may not care, but our clients will, and I definitely do. I've spent my life ensuring the Dixon name lives up to its heritage, and that includes having integrity and only working with the best."

Alex noticed that as Becca talked, her eyes bored into Dixon's head. He sat a few rows away. Alex tried to study him without the influence of her uncomfortable interactions with him. Distinguished in the way only the very wealthy can be, he lounged with his feet on the bench, taking up the whole row. He lifted his eyes from his phone and returned Becca's glare. She pasted a smile on her face. "Eric," she called. "Why don't you come over here and tell them all about the importance of integrity to the Dixon name?"

Dixon continued to stare before relaxing his face. He got up slowly, then sat across the aisle, facing them with his elbows on his knees. "Integrity is everything to Dixon Kitchens," he intoned. There was no conviction behind it, Alex thought. He was merely repeating a company line, one that had probably been drilled into him. His next words confirmed it. "My father always said that. 'Integrity is everything to Dixon Kitchens. Without integrity, we are nothing but manufacturers. And we are, my son, much more than manufacturers. We are dreams. We are hopes. We are the foundation.'" Dixon shook his head with a smirk. "If I had a dime for every time I heard that—oh wait, I do!"

Alex felt Becca stiffen. William's chin dropped. Alex's attempt at impartiality vaporized; the more she was around Dixon, the less she liked him, and she didn't like him to begin with.

"They had some questions about the vetting process for the chefs," Becca said. "I assured them the selection by the judges is entirely independent. They don't even know whose food they're tasting until after they've made their selection."

"Absolutely," Dixon said. "Becca here insisted that we run this like a real cooking show."

"Because it *is* a real cooking show," Becca hissed, then straightened. "*Dining + Destinations* is an authentic showcase of America's best talent in unique locations," she said.

"Whose idea was it?" William asked.

"Oh, this is all Becca. She's the brains behind the show." Dixon winked, making his compliment seem more like an indulgence. "I'm just the money man."

"Yes, and we are so grateful for that." Becca's voice dripped acid.

William cleared his throat. "It seems like you and MJ are on better terms this morning," he said.

The smirk fell off Dixon's face. He glared angrily at William, then gradually smiled. "She's a woman. She gets dramatic." He looked around the train. "Where is she?"

Becca rolled her eyes. "You didn't even notice that your nanny—I mean your host isn't here?" she asked. Dixon didn't answer. Instead, he thrust his hand and chin out, impatiently prompting her to continue. It was Becca's turn to smirk. "She missed the train."

"What?" Dixon shouted. He stood up. "Where's the conductor? We need to go back and get her."

Becca laughed. "They are not going to go back, Eric. Not even for you. In case you've forgotten, not only are we not the only ones on this train, but they also have a schedule to keep."

"I don't care," Dixon said, puffing up and craning his neck to search for the conductor. He saw her talking with the chefs. He started walking towards her. Becca grabbed his sleeve and yanked him back.

"Do not make a fool of yourself," Becca said. "I had a car waiting at the peak. MJ will be where she's supposed to be."

"She damn well better be," Dixon said. He stalked back to his seat and looked out the window. Alex doubted he saw any of the passing scenery.

William slumped back in his seat. "Whew! That was tense."

Becca waved her hand. "Day in the life," she said. "Don't you two worry. Everything's going to go smoothly tonight. Have you got your interviews lined up?"

"I've got appointments with Sergio and LuEllen this afternoon, and Paul and Emily tomorrow," Alex answered.

"You're interviewing Emily?" William asked. "I wouldn't think you'd need to."

"Of course I am. I've talked with her as a friend, but as a journalist, I'll ask different questions. You know I'm a pro."

"Oh yes, no question about that," William said, then turned to Becca. "I've got the opposite schedule: Emily and Paul today, LuEllen and Sergio tomorrow. What about the judges?"

Becca consulted her phone. Alex could see she'd pulled up a calendar app. "I have you arriving at the showroom early tonight and you'll get a brief few minutes with each of them. There are three of them and twelve of you, so you two and four others will get ten minutes each tonight, then tomorrow the remaining six journalists will interview them." She paused. "I don't have to remind you of the NDA, do I?" she asked while going back and forth between them.

William was obviously offended. "As Alex said, we're pros. This is what we do. We understand, and signed an agreement to that effect, that anything we see, hear, taste, etc. this week is embargoed until Monday," he said stiffly.

Becca patted his knee. "No offense meant, young man."

He relaxed. "Well, because you called me young, you're forgiven."

The producer stood up. "If you'll excuse me, I have a few things to address with our camera crew before we pull into the station."

Alex put her fingers on the window, her eyes following a small stream as it tumbled down the mountain. She felt like that water, flowing around obstacles. When she pursued this assignment, she figured there'd be tension—it was a competition show, after all—but she thought it would be between the chefs, not the whole crew.

"You doing alright?" William asked.

"You always know, don't you?" Alex answered with her own question. "It's the drama. The tension. Him," she said, indicating Dixon. "I don't have the patience for it any more. Life's too short and you never know what's going to happen." She smiled shyly. "I am such a cliché, aren't I," she said. It wasn't a question.

"You're a powerhouse is what you are," William said, then reached across and squeezed her hand. "How's the rash doing?"

Alex pulled her other hand away from her neck. She hadn't even realized she'd been scratching. "Annoying as all get out. My doctor gave me a steroid cream, but it doesn't seem to do much but make my skin drier. I didn't even get radiation in that area, but it's still affected."

"The skin is your biggest organ," William said, then laughed. "I said organ." Alex rolled her eyes. "But seriously. It is one big organ, so while the radiation might have been concentrated in one area, I'm not surprised it's affecting you outside of that."

"Still stinks," Alex said. She continued to watch the slowly passing scenery. She felt like she could stick her hand out the window and brush the trees. It may have been three months since her last radiation treatment, but she'd put her body through the ringer. That's what happens when you have cancer.

Until her diagnosis the summer before, she'd had no idea what cancer meant. She'd heard of chemo and radiation, of course, but not what they *actually* meant. What a sentinel node was. Or an axillary node dissection. Or lymphedema, one of the possible re-sults of having nodes removed to see if they were also cancerous, or if it was just the lump in her breast. She didn't know what a port was, or that she'd have one installed above her heart so her nurses could more easily administer the cell-killing, life-saving drug. She rubbed the spot and felt the round piece of plastic, or whatever it was, underneath her skin, and the tube that connected the port to her veins.

"Is it bothering you?" William asked softly.

Alex turned her face towards him and gave him a tender smile. "Not really. It's still an anomaly. Feels weird knowing there's this foreign object in my body."

William squeezed her hand again. Alex appreciated he didn't try to commiserate, didn't offer platitudes. "When do you get it out?" he asked.

"I'm getting blood work done next week when I get back, and if my cancer markers are good, I should get it removed in a few weeks."

"Let me know the date and I'll come visit so we can celebrate. I might even bring Billy."

"Deal," Alex said. The train slowed to a stop. She scooted to the end of her row of seats so she could stand up without bumping into William. They filed into the aisle with the other passengers and she caught Emily's eye as everyone made their way to the center of the car to exit. Emily got off the train and waited to the side for Alex and William.

"Spill," William said as soon as he got to Emily. "What's the major malfunction between Mr. Clean Cut and Mr. Bad Boy?"

"Just boys and their toys," she said. When William raised his eyebrow, she explained. "They were arguing over knife manufacturers."

"I bet that was a sharp conversation," Alex said.

"I'm sure it was a real cut-up," William quipped.

Emily groaned. "Anyway, Sergio's all about Wüsthof and Paul swears by Shun." She shrugged. "Chefs. We do love our knives, that's for sure."

The trio fell in with the crowd of people departing the station and walked towards the parking lot and the waiting shuttle.

"I'm surprised you don't carry yours around with you all the time," William said.

"Who says I don't?" Emily winked, then nodded towards the other chefs. "I've got to sit with them again. Becca wants to keep the four of us together in some misguided attempt to get us to bond. Or she just wants more drama so Mike can capture it on camera." She quickly searched Alex's face. "You doing OK?"

Alex smiled. "You, too?" she saw the question on Emily's face. "William also asked. I didn't think I was being that obvious."

"It's obvious to people who love you. You're allowed to be upset, pissed even, you know," Emily said.

"I do," Alex said. "But I try to keep it under wraps when I'm working."

"You're human, my friend. William, keep on taking care of her. I've got to get back there." Emily walked towards the back of the shuttle and took a seat next to Paul.

Alex and William sat towards the front of the bus. William instinctively let her take the window seat. "She's a good egg, that one."

"Em?" Alex asked. "She sure is. I'm glad you two have finally met."

"It'll be fun to interview her this afternoon. Who are you talking to first?"

"Sergio. Should be interesting."

Chapter 6

Sergio sipped his tea. His movements were almost dainty, incongruous with his tattoos and scowl. He put the cup back into the saucer and placed his hands on the marble table, contemplating his fingers as he spread them. He began tapping his index finger, the nervous tic betraying him before he seemed to realize what he was doing and stopped.

"Did I always want to be a chef?" Sergio laughed, but it sounded hollow. "Yes."

Alex waited for him to continue. Silence was usually her best interviewing technique, but Sergio seemed to be one of those rare people who didn't feel the need to fill the gap. "What's your first memory of cooking?" she prompted.

Sergio didn't answer right away. This seemed like a pretty innocuous question and she wondered why he was so hesitant. He took a breath and sat back, appraising her. "You and Emily are close," he said.

"Yes. We're neighbors."

He cocked his head. "You're more than that."

Alex nodded. She knew exactly what Sergio was doing and decided to let him. "Absolutely. She was my lifeline during my treatments."

"She's intense."

"You have no idea!" Alex laughed. "Or maybe you do. It seems like you two have met before."

Sergio nodded. "We have similar interests."

"Are you part of the chef-farmer coalition she founded?"

"Charter member," Sergio said. "When I heard some pink-haired cook up in Chicago wanted to create a co-op between chefs and small farmers, I was all-in."

"That's been what, ten years now?"

"Twelve. We've done a lot of good, saved a lot of farms. Even helped enact some legislation to thwart those giant corporations and their predatory practices." His eyes flared, and Alex saw the same passion in him she saw in Emily.

"I know why Em is so dedicated. Why are you?"

Sergio took another sip of his tea, his eyes peering at Alex over the rim of the fine china cup. "My step-father was the CEO of one of those giant corporations." He gently set the cup back in the saucer. "You asked about my first memory of cooking? I was five. Mom and I had gone to the farmer's stand down the road and bought a bunch of fresh spinach. She put a skillet on the stove and a stepstool in front of it and handed me a bottle of olive oil. I poured way too much in there, but she simply smiled at me and poured a little back out. She turned the burner on low and threw in some garlic she'd diced. I didn't quite have my legendary knife skills yet." He looked off in the distance. Alex knew he wasn't with her anymore. He was standing on a stepstool in front of a pan shimmering with oil.

"Once we could smell the garlic–I can still smell it, you know–she handed me the bowl of spinach and told me to throw it in. I looked at her like she was crazy. There was no way we could eat that much spinach." Sergio smiled.

"I have to ask," Alex said. "Spinach?"

"I know, not what you'd expect from a five-year-old, right? Mom had a rule: try everything once. If I didn't like it, I didn't have to eat it. Turns out I loved sauteed spinach. I'd never seen her make it, though. Watching that huge pile of leaves wilt down into a dish I loved was magic."

Alex watched Sergio's face transform. He lit up from within. His frown smoothed away and his entire body relaxed.

"Mom sprinkled a little kosher salt and ground some pepper, and we sat in the formal dining room eating spinach I'd sauteed on fine china. To this day, it's still the best spinach I've ever had."

"How long has she been gone?" Alex asked gently.

The wistful smile disappeared. "Too long." He stopped and Alex waited. This time, Sergio filled the silence. "She died when I was away. Robert sent me to a private boarding school. That's what you did when you were a big corporate muckety-muck."

From the research she'd done on the chefs before arriving in Colorado Springs, Alex knew Robert was Sergio's step-father. She waited to see what more he would tell her.

Sergio wrapped both hands around the teacup. Alex was afraid it would shatter under his grip. "I'd come home for holidays and summer, and Mom would try to visit during the school year, but Robert wanted her all to himself."

"You were an only child, I take it?"

"Yes. Then Mom died, and it was just him and me. And then it was just me."

Alex gave him a moment, and then asked: "What happened?"

Sergio barked out a laugh. "Oh, you mean you haven't heard? I thought everyone knew. I know for damn sure that's part of why I'm on this show. I'm the Bad Boy, capital Bs."

"I know the official bio. I'd like to hear about it from you, if you'll tell me. If not, that's fine, too. I respect your desire for privacy."

"What kind of journalist are you?" Sergio said. "No offense. Emily's told me enough about you." He waved his hand. "I haven't had privacy since they arrested me.

"Sixteen," he continued. "I was sixteen. I knew Mom wasn't happy. When it was just the two of us, she'd be light as air. Laughing, free. But when he was around she'd shrink. It was like she'd disappear. Looking back, all the signs were there, but I was a teenage boy, you know? I was more interested in sports and girls than I was trying to figure out what was going on with my mother.

"Then I got the call. Mom had fallen down the stairs. Yeah, right. I knew that bastard had killed her. I came home for the funeral and hid in the attic. We had this sprawling monstrosity, of course, and the attic was like a football field. I found Mom's journals." A tear slid down Sergio's cheek. He let it. "I confronted Robert. He denied it; said Mom had had a vivid imagination. I threatened to go to the police. He hit me. I hit back."

Alex held her breath, afraid to move.

"We were in the kitchen. He lunged at me and I grabbed a knife from the block on the counter and held it, pointing towards him. He fell on it.

"I spent the next year in juvie while they figured out it was self-defense. The one good thing that came out of it was they put me in the kitchen."

"And that's where you found your love of cooking?"

"Not at first. In fact, I got into quite a bit of trouble," Sergio said. This was news to Alex. Since juvenile records were sealed, she only knew that he'd been arrested for murder and then acquitted a year later.

"What kind of trouble?"

"Nothing major. It was more quantity than quality. Wouldn't make my bed. Wouldn't show up to class. Wouldn't do my homework. Truth is, I was spending every minute outside, and then in the kitchen. We had a guy in there–Enrique–he was a magician. Here I was in juvie, but I was eating some of the best food in Asheville, and that's saying something. He'd been in a similar situation as mine, except he wasn't acquitted. He kind of took me under his wing, showed me how to combine flavors and textures. Showed me how to use a knife."

"I have to say, I'm a bit surprised they let you use one, considering why you were there in the first place."

"Ha!" Sergio said. "I can see why Em likes you. That was all Enrique. Said he wanted to show me how to use a knife as a tool, not as a weapon."

"That succeeded," Alex said. "I noticed you never went to culinary school."

"Let's just say I never paid tuition, but I certainly went to school," he said, pushing his now-empty teacup to the side of the table. "Although my wages were either nonexistent or so low it seemed like I was paying for it."

"The privilege of staging with the best, right?"

"You got it. I had to work another job. Slept in my car at times." Sergio shrugged. "When you find out what you're supposed to do with your life, you do what you have to do to make it happen."

Alex knew all about that. She'd paid her own dues, working dinner shifts at a restaurant, then overnights at the paper. She needed the tips to pay her student loans, and shift meals at the restaurant meant she didn't have to buy as many groceries. Then when she made the switch to travel writer, she had a couple lean years before she built her audience enough to secure advertising on her site.

She wouldn't change a thing.

"I'd do it all again," Sergio said, echoing her thought.

"How'd you hear about *Dining + Destinations*?" Alex asked.

"They invited me. Apparently Dixon had his salespeople scouting out kitchens that had good press but could use a refresh. Sob stories, you know, like Emily's and mine."

"How did that make you feel? Did you feel used?"

His eyes drilled into hers and held them. "You do what you have to do."

Alex stepped outside to get a breath of fresh air. She had a few minutes before her interview with LuEllen and she needed to shift gears from her intense conversation with Sergio. He was much more open than she figured he would be, considering his gruff demeanor.

She closed her eyes and inhaled deeply, catching a whiff of the waffle cones made fresh in the ice cream shop. The sky was bright blue, and the reflection of the building across the pond shimmered in the water.

"Ms. Paige?"

Alex turned to see LuEllen. "We've climbed Pikes Peak together; you can call me Alex," she smiled. "The weather is so nice; much warmer than this morning. Should we sit out here?" Alex asked.

"That would be lovely, my dear. Thank you."

The two women sat at one of the empty wrought-iron tables. LuEllen leaned back in her chair and sighed. "What a view," she said. "Not a darn thing like what I see back home."

"You're on the Gulf, right?"

"Sure am. Gulf Shores, Alabama, to be exact. Got me a little shrimp shack on the beach. I named it LuEllen's Shrimp Shack. I'm creative like that," LuEllen winked.

Alex laughed. "A spot on the beach? Sounds lovely."

"Best sunsets you ever saw. Sunrises, too. This here is pretty, and that view from up top was sure something, but there's nothing like my sandy paradise."

"What brought you here?" Alex asked.

"Ambition," LuEllen replied, surprising Alex. The older woman caught the fleeting look on the reporter's face. "What, a sweet little old lady like me isn't supposed to be ambitious?"

"No, it's not that at all. I appreciate the candor."

"I want a line of LuEllen's Shrimp Shacks surrounding the Gulf of Mexico, from South Padre Island to Key West. A partnership with Dixon Kitchens can make that happen."

"You've been around for quite some time, haven't you?" Alex asked.

"Now young lady, are you picking on my age?" LuEllen smiled as she said it.

Alex laughed. "Not at all. In fact," she said, studying her, "I don't think you're that much older than I am."

"A southern lady never divulges her age," LuEllen said.

"Have you always known you wanted to be a chef?" Alex asked, repeating the question she'd asked Sergio.

"Heavens no," LuEllen said. "Cooking was the last thing on my mind. I lived on ramen soup and peanut butter. Not together, mind you," she chuckled. "I wanted to be an engineer. Put myself through school, racked up student loans in the triple digits, and when I finally got a job in my field, they paid a pittance. Had to work in a restaurant at night to make ends meet."

"Did you wait tables?"

"Oh no. I'm not that much of a people person." LuEllen laughed at Alex's expression. "Hard to believe, right?" She shrugged. "When you're in this business as long as I've been, you learn. No, I stayed out of sight. Got a job in the kitchen at my uncle's spot. Only one who would hire me, but he'd always had a soft spot for me."

LuEllen stopped and stared at the mountain in the distance. A hard look came over her face.

"What happened?" Alex asked softly.

"I learned how to cook, that's what happened," the chef said, still looking towards the peak.

Alex knew the subject was closed. This was one person definitely immune to her special talent for extracting secrets and stories. She switched gears. "What would winning a new kitchen mean to you?"

"I already answered that. It would mean a partnership, which would mean a whole chain of restaurants in my name."

"You sound pretty certain about that."

LuEllen fixed her ice blue eyes on Alex. "I didn't get this far by not knowing what I want, and not knowing how to get it."

Alex shivered. This woman had reserves that frightened her. She reminded Alex of her old editor. Hard. Determined. Often rude and cutthroat. To him, all that mattered was getting the story. To LuEllen, all that mattered was getting her chain of restaurants.

LuEllen smiled, a sweet, benign smile that broke the tension. "Oh my," she tittered and patted Alex's hand. "I do get a bit dramatic, don't I?" LuEllen looked at her watch, a slim activity tracker with a rose gold band. "Would you look at that? I better get a move on. I don't want the shuttle to leave without me." She stood up and gathered the large purse she'd set on the chair beside her. "I'll see you at Dixon's showroom shortly, my dear. Just wait 'til you taste what I've got cooking for you."

Alex stood up with her and watched LuEllen shuffle through the glass doors towards the lobby. She felt distinctly unsettled. Her conversation with Sergio had been dramatic, but that was because the man had led a dramatic life. It sounded like LuEllen had, too, but the tension from that conversation came from the woman herself, not from her story. "She's one to watch," Alex muttered to herself, then shook it off and entered the hotel.

Chapter 7

Alex turned right and walked towards the open doors to The Hotel Bar. William rested his elbows on the polished mahogany bar, flirting with Max, the same bartender from the night before. Max wore a white tuxedo shirt and black tie and maneuvered a silver martini shaker in an elegant figure eight, then poured brown liquid into a chilled glass holding a skewer of nearly black cherries.

"Manhattan?" Alex asked.

"But of course. When in Colorado Springs..."

"That makes absolutely no sense."

"I know. Isn't it delightful?" William leaned to take a sip of his drink so it wouldn't spill over the edge, then scooted it closer to him.

"I take it your interviews went well?" Alex asked, then pointed at William's drink when the bartender caught her eye.

"Emily's did. I adore that woman."

"How could you not?" Alex asked. The bartender poured her drink to the rim and pushed it towards her, somehow managing not to spill a drop. She took a sip and gave him a big smile. "Delicious."

"I'll say," William replied, then switched back to Emily. "I just love her passion. To give up a high-faluting lawyer gig to slog in a kitchen? She must really love cooking."

"I can verify that. But seriously, can you imagine Em in a suit all day, writing up arguments and dealing with judges and juries and, worse, other attorneys?"

"The arguments, yes, I can totally see her arguing, and I'd be afraid to be opposing counsel. The rest? No way." He swiveled his barstool to look out the floor-to-ceiling windows across the room. "I love the name of this place," he said.

"The Hotel Bar?" Alex asked.

"Yes. It's so... pretentious without seeming pretentious. *We're The Broadmoor*," he intoned in a terrible British accent. "*We don't need to come up with some fancy name. When you're at The Broadmoor, you drink at The Hotel Bar.*"

Alex giggled. "That is the worst accent I think I've ever heard. What was that supposed to be, anyway?"

William put his hand on his chest and gasped. "Oh my. How dare you not recognize my upper crust upbringing through the dulcet tones of my obviously superior education. Pshaw. I demand an immediate apology." He broke out in a grin and the two touched their glasses together, the fine crystal ringing like a bell.

"How much did Emily tell you about why she opened her own place?" Alex asked.

"All of it. Or at least, enough to paint a picture. Farmer's daughter, corporate bullies stole their farm, which basically killed her parents, so she took a sabbatical and spent all her time cooking. Turned out she was good at it. Like, really good at it."

Alex nodded. She and Emily had had several conversations about the routes they'd each taken to find their passions. "It's why

she'll only work with small farmers. Don't even think of mention-
ing those huge conglomerates unless you want to see fireworks."

"Is that why her hair's fuchsia?"

"Funny man. Seriously, though. She lists the farms she works
with on her menu and website. Buying direct makes her food costs
higher, but because she's in Lincoln Park she can charge more. It's
also part of why her kitchen's in such sad shape."

"Can't afford the new equipment?"

Alex tilted her glass at him. "Bingo. She really needs to expand;
her reservations are booked for months and she practically had a
riot on her hands when she announced she would be closed this
week. But the equipment she needs is so expensive, and she needs
all of it."

"All of it?"

"Yep. She got the restaurant for a song. It had been a fami-
ly-owned diner for decades, but the last generation didn't want
it, so they neglected it before deciding to sell." Alex took another
sip. "So what about Paul? He seems a little, I don't know."

William nodded. "He's very much *I don't know*. An enigma, if
you will. You'll probably get more out of him than I did. But first I
want to hear about Sexy Sergio. Did you get Mr. Gruff-and-Tum-
ble to open up?"

Alex grinned. "A good reporter never tells."

"That is the exact opposite of how it works," William said.

Alex winked and then responded carefully. "He's a deep one."

"Deep as in complex or deep as in drama?"

"Yes," she said. "He had a rough childhood, but ended up finding
a mentor. I'm sure he'll tell you about it when you talk to him
tomorrow."

"Care to give me any insight?"

Alex ran her finger around the rim of her martini glass, a thoughtful expression on her face. "He's passionate. I mean, they're all passionate, but he's got this drive that seems like it almost consumes him. Kind of like Emily's. In fact, in many ways, he's a lot like Em."

"Do you think he can win?"

"I hate to say it, because you know who my favorite is, but yes. He's got that something, you know?" She plucked a cherry off the spear and popped it in her mouth. "What about Paul? How did he strike you?"

William took a long sip of his cocktail. "He's an odd one," he finally said.

"You don't like him."

"I've only talked to the man once, but there's something off. He's definitely got a chip on his shoulder."

"About what?"

"The competition, for one. He loathes Sergio, thinks LuEllen's a hack, and dismissed Em like she's a flash in the pan," William explained.

Alex's eyes flared. "*Elements* has been one of the top restaurants in one of the top culinary cities in the world for more than a decade," she said, defending her friend.

"Yeah, well, Paul seems to think Chicago's all pizza and hot dogs and wouldn't know an amuse-bouche if it hit the city in the head."

Alex laughed. "Won't he be surprised when Emily trounces him."

William drummed his fingers on the bar. "It'll certainly be interesting. He's obviously got skills or he wouldn't be here. But there's something under the surface, something simmering, if you will, but he tries to push it off with this veneer. I don't buy it. He seems to be driven purely by narcissism, by a need to prove something. He's arrogant, and he's dismissive."

"Sounds like you two had one heck of a conversation."

"I wouldn't call it so much a conversation as a lecture." William shuddered. "I'm glad we're not judging, because he'd lose on personality alone."

Alex considered what William said. He assessed people quickly and was usually spot on. He took an immediate disliking to her ex, and after discovering William was right about Ben, she noticed he was often right about everyone else. For him to feel so strongly about Paul after a brief interview gave her pause.

"I wonder what you'll think of LuEllen," Alex mused.

"Oh?"

"She's also, forceful, shall we say. There's a lot going on with her."

"I suppose you could say that about anyone. So she's not quite the doting grandmotherly type she appears to be?"

"I'll have to let you discover that for yourself," Alex winked, then finished her Manhattan, "because it's time to go see these chefs in action. You ready?"

"To eat? Always."

Alex considered the dynamics of the four chefs and wondered what the evening's competition would be like. She imagined it would be fierce. These were four people who, for various reasons, desperately wanted to win. How far would they go to make that happen?

Chapter 8

The Dixon Kitchens showroom sat in a prime location with a view of Pikes Peak. It looked like someone's home. A massive home, but a home nonetheless. Alex entered a black and white tiled foyer through the tall, heavy double doors made of solid cherry. The room to the right was outfitted as an upscale residential kitchen, and to the left was a large living room with a fireplace, several seating areas, and tables strewn with catalogs. A wide corridor divided the structure, and she followed it towards the back of the house. She noticed a hall to the right behind the residential kitchen. Alex figured it led to offices and storerooms. She returned her attention to the main hallway. It was lined with photo after photo of Dixon with chefs. She recognized several of them. Some of the photos, obviously taken long ago, included an older man that Alex assumed was Dixon's father, the man who'd founded the company.

The hallway opened up to a giant space with floor to ceiling windows. Alex gasped. The sun was still high enough to burnish the red slabs of Garden of the Gods.

"Magnificent, isn't it?"

Alex turned her head and reared back. The man obviously had no sense of personal space. Put him with Harriet and they'd probably be stuck together like velcro. "Yes, Mr. Dixon. Stunning. You must be very proud."

"Call me Eric. It's all part of the show," he said, gesturing to the room. They'd broken the large space up into four commercial kitchen areas, showcasing some of the different configurations they offered. "And this week, I mean that literally," he chuckled, then took a sip from his highball. Alex could smell an energy drink and figured he'd laced it liberally with vodka.

Becca approached them. "Eric, we need to discuss a couple of items for tonight," she said, then turned to Alex. "Hello; I trust your interviews went well this afternoon?"

"Yes, and I'm looking forward to talking with the judges."

The producer consulted her watch. "We'll get those started shortly." Becca grabbed the attention of a passing server. "Get her something to drink, please. Prosecco?" she asked, and Alex nodded.

"And one for me, too," William said as he reached Alex's side.

Dixon scowled and abruptly backed away. He turned to Becca. "Let's go. I'm sure you've got plenty of i's to dot." He winked at Alex, scowled at William again, and walked towards a swinging door tucked in between two of the show kitchens. He stopped first in front of MJ, who was leaning against one of the stainless steel islands and talking with Mike. At Dixon's gesture, she pulled a tall frosted glass bottle from a cabinet and refilled his drink. Alex's guess had been correct.

Becca stared after him, then gave William and Alex a false smile. "I'll be back shortly to get you started with your interviews. Please enjoy the view and the prosecco until then," she said, then crossed the room to the door.

Alex followed Becca to a semi-circular booth. "Stellar? This is Alex Paige, our Chicago-based journalist. Alex, Stellar Evans. Just a reminder that you've only got ten minutes. I want to make sure everyone interviews the judges."

Stellar extended her hand to Alex and the two women shook. The judge scooted around the side of the booth so they could sit across from each other, and Alex slid into the banquette.

"Since we don't have much time, I'll dive right in. What brings you here?"

Stellar pointed towards Becca. "That woman right there. She's the heart, soul, and brains of Dixon Kitchens and if she asks me to do something, I do it."

"Have you known each other long?"

"Decades." Stellar smiled at Alex's raised eyebrow. "I know. I look fantastic, don't I? We went to school together. Two misfits who cared more about books than boys."

"Have you stayed in touch ever since?"

"No. We moved to D.C. when I was a teenager and she and I lost touch. But then, I opened a restaurant, she took over the family business, and we reconnected."

"Family business?"

"You didn't know? Becca's a Dixon. She's his half-sister." Stellar pointed behind Alex and she turned to see Eric Dixon, who was leaning on one of the granite-topped islands with a drink in his hand. "Hard to believe they're related," Stellar said with a shake of her head. "She got all the brains; he got all the BS."

Alex really, really wanted to dig deeper into that topic, but she knew she didn't have much time. Maybe she'd find out more over the next couple of days. "I know you've judged several cooking competitions, including some pretty high-profile shows. What makes this one different?"

"Great question, and nice to know you've done your homework. D and D is about the food, yes, but it's also about the place. I love the concept of showcasing unique destinations and local and regional cuisine."

"That's what drew me, too," Alex said. "I believe every place has a story, and local cuisine evolves based on what's available."

"Exactly. I also love that every chef walks away with something and there's none of this shaming crap that happens on so many other shows. We all need some feel good entertainment right now, and the way Becca pitched it, this show is all about feeling good."

"And tasting good, too."

"Exactly!" Stellar said, and patted her stomach. "I earned these curves."

Alex laughed with her. "Have you talked to Becca about a D.C. episode?"

"Yes, I sure have. She's going to see how this pilot goes and then we'll talk."

"Washington's not exactly known as a culinary town. Except for your restaurant, of course."

"Exactly," Stellar said again. "And I aim to change that." She launched into a passionate description of her plans for elevating the restaurant scene in the nation's capital.

"Sorry to interrupt, but it's time to move on," Becca said while approaching the booth.

Stellar reached into her clutch and extracted a business card, passing it to Alex. "We have more to discuss, I believe. Feel free to call me any time."

Alex accepted the card with a smile and followed Becca to another booth. William stood up and stepped away from the table. He faced Alex, his back to the judge and to Becca, and mimicked gagging. Alex stifled a smile. Becca introduced her to a short man with a balding pate sitting in the center of the semi-circular booth. When it became obvious that he wasn't going to move, Alex sat down on the edge.

Alex studied the man. He was small, compact, yet seemed to fill the entire booth. She waited. He stared at his phone, tapping rapidly with his thumbs. She'd read several of his restaurant reviews, and her eyes fairly burned from his searing criticism. In the decades he'd been covering the food scene, he'd written one positive review. One. The rest were variations on a misanthropic theme.

If Alex still worked for a newspaper, she'd have to approach the man as a disinterested observer. She would have launched into asking questions. She instinctively disliked the man, which meant her writing would have been dispassionate. Dull, even. Now, however, she answered to no one but her readers, and they respected her opinions. They expected her passion and her insight. So, she waited. From what she'd gleaned about Arnold Abbot, she knew he craved recognition and publicity. Any kind of publicity. Alex had a feeling that meant his rudeness was carefully curated to get him the most ink.

"Are you just going to sit there and watch me or are you actually going to conduct an interview?" Abbot asked without a break in his typing.

"I can wait until you're done," Alex said.

"Don't we only have ten minutes?" He continued typing.

"Yes. But please, I don't want to interrupt." Alex gestured to his phone and smiled, which Abbot missed because his gaze was still focused on the screen in his hands. "Obviously whatever you're doing is more important."

Abbot sighed, put his phone down on the table, and snapped at a passing server. "You. Bring me another," he said, pointing to his half-full rocks glass. He glanced at Alex. "You're the blogger," he stated. "Ask your silly questions and let's get on with it."

Alex simmered, but she did not respond. Her years as an investigative journalist had taught her the best way to react to bullies was to ignore them. "You've been a food critic for quite some time."

"Decades. Yes. Did you have a question, or didn't they teach you how to interview in blogging school?"

"In all those years, it seems, based on your reviews, you only found one restaurant you liked. Why do you keep doing it?"

Abbot drained his glass and searched the room until he located the server. He snapped his fingers and motioned the young man to hurry up. "Because they need to know someone's watching. They need to know they can't put swill on a plate and call it caviar. They need to know they'll be held accountable. They need to know there are standards." The server placed a fresh cocktail in front of him and Abbot gulped a third of it.

"And the one place that did meet your standards? What separated it?"

"That was thirty years ago. You expect me to remember that?"

"If that's the only positive review you've given a restaurant over a career of offering scathing opinions, then yes, I do expect you to remember it." Alex watched him. The chef who'd received his rare praise had been a young woman at the time. Abbot's review was such a rarity it had propelled her into the national spotlight, catapulting her restaurant's success. She'd been at the top ever since. "Especially since she also happens to be a fellow judge."

Abbot clenched his fists and directed his glare towards Dixon. He still hadn't looked at Alex. "Stellar Evans has no place here. Neither does that fru-fru do-nothing whatever you call it. I told Dixon he needed judges of higher caliber, but he decided to cater to the lowest common denominator. Just like those four," he said, waving to the curtain hiding the chefs while they prepped the evening's dinner.

"You don't like chefs, do you?" Alex asked.

Abbot fully looked at Alex for the first time. "No, I don't," he said. "They're arrogant. They're controlling. They're entitled. *Yes, chef. No, chef.* Ridiculous. They make food. They're not saving lives. Yet they have a God complex to rival that of surgeons and dictators."

"Some would say the same of you. In fact, some have."

Abbot stared at her, then threw his head back and laughed. It was a high pitched laugh that set her nerves on edge. He shook his head and looked at Alex again. "Nobody has ever had the gumption to say that to my face. Sure, they've written it, but to look me in the eyes and tell me I'm a hypocrite?" He studied her. "You're a clever one, aren't you."

"I see things, that's all."

"And say them, too, apparently."

"What does it feel like, knowing you have the power to make or break someone's career? Playing God?" Alex knew she was pushing it, but this man, this hypocrite, as he so accurately worded it, irritated her to no end.

The corners of his mouth upturned ever so slightly as he gazed into the distance. He brought his eyes back to the table. Alex's notebook and poised pen must have registered, because a mask came over his face. "I do not 'play God,'" he said, using air quotes around the two words. "I inform the public about a chef's successes and shortcomings. The former are few; the latter are common."

"Since you dislike chefs, what prompted you to be a judge for this show, which seems to be centered more on celebrating than condemning?" Alex asked. She anticipated his answer and began writing before he spoke. Alex had a talent for looking people in the eye while taking notes, so they often didn't realize what she was doing, even though they knew they were being interviewed.

"Because I was their only choice. No other local critic, no other regional critic, no other national critic even comes close." Alex allowed herself a small smile. She'd written: *Best—only one*.

"Is that why you've won so many journalism awards?"

Abbot glared. "We're done here."

"Yes, you are. Time's up," Becca said as she approached the table. Her eyes darted between the critic and the journalist. "Did you two have a nice chat?"

"Oh yes," Alex said. "It was quite illuminating." She stood up. Since she'd been sitting so close to the edge of the booth she barely had to scoot over. "Mr. Abbot, thank you for the insightful discussion." She began walking away before the critic could respond. As they neared the last judge's table, she paused to reset herself.

"He has that effect on people," Becca commiserated.

"Vile man," Alex said under her breath, then spoke louder. "I suppose he'll make for some good tension for the show."

Becca refrained from commenting. "I think you'll like your next conversation."

Chapter 9

They reached the last booth as William stood up. The judge who'd been sitting across from him also stood, extending a manicured hand. William kissed it gently, his eyes shining. A server holding a tray of glasses approached and Alex grabbed two glasses, handing one to William.

"Oh, darling, you have rescued my parched palate," William said as he took the proffered glass from Alex. "My dear, have you met Jo?"

The judge turned, a graceful movement accompanied by a gentle swaying of chandelier earrings the size of dinner plates. As Alex shook her hand, she noticed the two inch nails decorated with various fruits. "I've not had the pleasure. Nice to meet you."

"Jo here's one of the judges, you know," William said. "Of course you know. Did you know she's got, what is it, three million followers? Phenomenal." William stared at the celebrity. He'd told Alex that one of the things that made him decide he'd cover this event, besides knowing that Alex would be there, was that one of his favorite influencers would be judging, completing the three C's: Chef, Critic, and Celebrity.

"Something like that," Jo said in a slightly husky voice.

"I've made some of your recipes," Alex said, and Jo's face lit up. "They're so simple and fast. How do you come up with them?"

Jo shrugged. "It's out of necessity, really. Putting all this together takes time." The lanky judge drew her hands down her body. "I needed to make something quickly before a show, decided to do it live, and people ate it up."

"Literally!" William quipped, and laughed at his own joke. "Well, not quite literally, because they didn't eat your video, but they made what you made and ate it."

Alex stared at William. Who was this flustered person? She'd known William was a big fan of the former drag performer turned celebrity chef, but she had no idea how much of a fan.

Becca's head darted back and forth, following the conversation. "Looks like you've got this covered. William, come with me. Stellar's next."

"You'll love her," Alex whispered to William as he passed, his eyes still focused on Jo.

"Shall we?" Jo sat at one end of the semi-circular booth and invited Alex to sit across from her.

From Alex's seat she could see William greet Stellar in the far booth. In between, Harriet sat with a look of horror as she listened to Abbot. Harriet glanced her way and mouthed, "Is he for real?" Alex stifled a laugh.

"Let me guess," Jo said, without looking behind. "One of your colleagues is currently held captive by our curmudgeonly critic."

"*Curmudgeonly* is one way to put it."

"Trust me, I have stronger words to use, but I've decided to be on my best behavior this week."

"Have you had the, ahem, *distinct pleasure* of previously encountering Mr. Abbot?"

Jo laughed, a deep, throaty rumble. "Not in the flesh. The poor man tried to eviscerate me on social, but my legion of Jolly Rogers made him walk the plank," she said, pronouncing the Jo- in jolly like her name.

"Jo-lly Rogers. You've got your own band of pirates, eh?"

"Sure do. Self-appointed take-no-prisoners defenders of yours truly."

"How'd that come about?" Alex asked. She'd known about Jo's legion of fans, whose dedication ranked with Taylor Swift's *Swifties* and Lady Gaga's *Little Monsters*, but she wondered how a person could earn such rabid fandom.

Jo smiled with a touch of sadness. "It began in your city, actually. I was scheduled to perform at the Baton Club when a band of self-righteous hypocritical do-gooders decided people like me needed to be taught a lesson. They literally set one of my friends on fire. Said she was going to hell anyway, they were just helping her along. They called her a 'flamer;' called it poetic justice."

Alex could practically feel the searing heat from Jo's memories when the realization hit her. "That was you? I remember that story. You saved her."

Jo shrugged dismissively. "Fire 101: smother it. I wore a cape as part of my costume."

"You're a hero."

"I'm a survivor."

Alex studied her. "I see why William adores you. As do many others."

Jo leaned back and took a deep breath. "I didn't set out for all this to happen. I simply loved performing. That night, before I got to the club, was the first time I posted a cooking video. One of the people who was waiting to get into the show when those awful people attacked my friend saw it. They reposted the video with what had happened that night."

"I can't believe I didn't make the connection."

"It was last summer, my dear. Didn't you have something else occupying you at the time?"

Alex laughed ruefully. "You might say that. How'd you know?"

Jo pointed to her own head. "The hair. I've had a few friends go through chemo. It's coming back nicely, by the way."

"Thank you. Now, we don't have much more time, so I suppose I should ask you about the show. Why did you say yes to being a judge? I'm assuming they asked you, or did you pursue it?"

"No, they came to me. Becca did. Frankly, I think she did it to spite her brother."

"Half-brother," Becca said, appearing behind Alex.

Jo smiled. "Half-brother. Anyway, she asked, I leapt. I realize I've become a bit of a figurehead for people who don't want to conform to self-righteous hypocritical do-gooders' ideas of who people should be. A show like this, produced by a big name like Dixon with an avowed playboy front and center could do a lot to help normalize accepting people for who they are. If Eric Dixon's okay with someone like me, we must have something worth sharing."

"She's right," Becca said to Alex. "I invited Jo specifically be-cause I knew Eric would hate it, but by the time he found out, the contract was signed." She turned to Jo. "I also invited you because I adore you."

"Mutual, love, mutual."

"Alex, we've got a few minutes before everything begins. Why don't you enjoy the view," Becca said. It was more of a directive than a suggestion.

Alex stood up and reached out her hand to shake Jo's again and Becca slid into her place in the booth. Alex walked towards the terrace, joining William as he exited Stellar's booth. He glanced back at Abbot and shook his entire body. "Ick ick ick," he said. "That man is pure ick."

They walked through the twelve-foot glass doors that had been secured open to allow easy access to the terrace. Rattan couches and chairs clustered around gas fire pits. A fountain designed to replicate a waterfall gurgled in one corner, and an empty stage occupied another.

Alex leaned on the railing, marveling at the striking contrast of the peaks of the Front Range and the red slabs jutting from the earth.

"Gorgeous. Simply gorgeous," William said as he leaned against the railing next to her. Alex turned her head to see he wasn't looking at the mountains. Instead, he was following Sergio on the large screen that had been placed outside. Mike and Dennis had trained cameras on the chefs' stations so attendees could watch them preparing the meals from the terrace. Dali's melting clock dripped down Sergio's arm and the timepiece's hands seemed to move as he deftly diced shallots. He swept the alliums to the side, then threw his knife up in the air. It flipped end over end. He reached up, grabbed the handle, and began dicing garlic. He looked at the camera and winked.

"Showoff," William said. "I love it."

"He's not the jerk I first thought he was," Alex said.

"Which is good, since he seems to have eyes for Emily."

Alex switched her gaze to watch Emily, whose station was next to Sergio's. Emily whisked ingredients in a glass bowl while slowly pouring a stream of what Alex guessed was extra virgin olive oil. On Emily's other side, Paul gently stirred something in a double boiler. Alex's stomach grumbled.

She felt bad for the judges. Well, two of them, anyway. They had to remain in their booths instead of being able to go outside. Curtains blocked their view of the chefs so they wouldn't know who made each course, and with a screen on the terrace, they were stuck waiting.

The show's concept appealed to Alex: the chef restaurateurs represented different regions of the country. For four nights in a row, they'd each prepare a different course of a four-course meal. The judges would vote on their favorite course each night. Instead of eliminating contestants, like so many food competition shows did, the chefs would be awarded prizes of varying size based on how many courses they'd won. The final dinner would take place at a unique destination. This inaugural show's setting: Garden of the Gods in Colorado Springs.

Alex knew Emily had to win. She simply couldn't afford to replace her stove, refrigerator, walk-in, and everything else at the same time. If she won, her restaurant would be entirely outfitted in new Dixon appliances, widely considered the best and a necessity for any serious chef. Emily had coveted their range for years and littered her home with catalogs marked with post-it flags. Unfortunately, their price was commensurate with their quality.

Dixon approached the stage, pulling the microphone from its stand. MJ walked up next to him, handing him a full drink. "Good to see she made it back," William whispered out of the side of his mouth. "Can't imagine Dixon is too thrilled with her," he said, emphasizing the first syllable of the name.

Alex stifled a laugh. Whenever she and William were together, she felt like they were two kids sitting in the back of the classroom, about to be sent to detention.

"Good evening, everyone. Welcome to *Dining + Destinations*," Dixon said, pronouncing the plus sign. "I hope you enjoyed your trip to the peak this morning, and it's good to see everyone made it down." He patted MJ on the shoulder. "Just kidding, MJ. It happens to the best of us. Well, not me, but it happens.

"Anywho, I think we're all looking forward to tonight's dinner. MJ, want to take it from here?"

The show's host smiled. There was a reason Dixon selected her to host his show: she was stunning.

MJ moved so the mountains were behind her. Mike followed her and she focused on the video camera he'd pointed in her direction. "It's the first day in our competition featuring four of the best chefs in the country. I have a feeling we're in for a treat, and even if the food disappoints, this view definitely will not." She paused. Alex figured it was for editing purposes. Mike could split the video after that last phrase if they needed to.

MJ shifted her attention to the screen. Emily's profile appeared, her fuchsia hair standing proud. "Let's introduce our first chef. Don't let her colorful hair fool you; Ms. Kincaid is a classically trained chef whose resume includes stints at French Laundry and Alinea, among others. She's got quite the story, but I'll let her tell you herself."

Alex frowned. "She's going to hate that intro. The idea that someone would judge her competence based on her hairstyle infuriates her."

"As it should," William said. "All they have to do is taste her food and they'll forget all about it."

"That's the point. They shouldn't have to taste her food not to judge her." Alex glared at MJ. "And to have Miss America over there define her? Too much."

Chapter 10

The exterior of Emily's restaurant filled the screen. It was a tiny storefront; the picture windows framed by dark wood gave it the feel of a French bistro. They must have shot the video in May; tulips curved out of vases on the outdoor tables, and a row of colorful planters filled with daffodils lined the sidewalk. Above the door, *Elements* flowed in an elegant cursive. Alex knew the neon sign lit up at night with a soft, inviting glow. She'd sat in its light many a night while waiting for Emily before the two would head down to Coda for some live jazz.

The image on the screen switched to a montage of the interior of the restaurant. Emily at the host stand, talking to patrons, in the kitchen. The camera zeroed in for a close-up as she diced onions, her custom-made knife handles a blur of pink. The video and music faded to what looked like a talk show set. There was MJ, sitting in a red armchair, and across from her sat Emily in a yellow counterpart. Emily fidgeted, her fingers toying with the loose fabric of her floral pants.

"Emily," MJ began, leaning forward, "you left a successful career as an attorney to open your restaurant. Why?"

Alex could see Emily relax. She could talk about this all day. Her restaurant was her passion. "I like to eat," Emily said with a grin.

"So do I, but I can't see chucking all this," MJ waved at the microphone and the set, "to spend my days in a small room sweating while people yell at each other."

"Ah, see, there's the misconception. There's no yelling at *Elements*. I don't yell at my coworkers; they don't yell at me."

"And the customers? Surely you have to deal with a few irate patrons now and then."

"It's rare. Very, very rare. *Elements* is a happy place." Emily grinned again. Her face shone with excitement. "To answer your question, that's why. I love food. I love cooking. I love feeding people. It's my love language, as they say."

"You grew up on a farm, right?"

A shadow crossed Emily face and her lips relaxed into something less than a grin and not quite a frown. "Yes. It's a hard life. We raised cattle and grew corn, which meant we worked year round. I didn't leave my small town until I went to college. Never had the chance because mom and dad never got a break. It's why I'm so passionate about supporting small farms and producers. I didn't even know farm-to-table was a thing," Emily said, with a smile that lit up her eyes. "It's simply how I've always eaten, and how I've always cooked. When you grow up on a farm, that's just the way it is."

"Didn't you take one of those big corporate farms to court?"

"I represented a group of families whose livelihoods had been destroyed by predatory practices, yes," Emily said. "It's what made me decide to open my own place."

"Because you lost?" MJ prodded.

"No. Well, yes. I suppose you could put it that way." Alex could see Emily composing herself. She knew if her friend didn't, her rage would escape and she might not be selected for the show.

Although, with reality TV the way it was, they might have wanted a chef with pink hair and a blazing temper. "I took a sabbatical and cooked. For the next six months, all I did was cook. And I realized that I may not have wanted to live the farm life, but I could support those that do in a different way. So I quit law and opened *Elements*."

"Just like that, eh?" MJ smiled to take the sting out of her words. "So tell us, Emily; what would being on *Dining + Destinations* mean to you? You know that each of the four chefs we select will walk away with at least one new Dixon appliance. One will get a whole new kitchen."

Emily inhaled and looked up at the ceiling before lowering her gaze to look directly at MJ. "It would be a game changer. You've seen my kitchen." At this prompt, the screen switched to video of the cramped space. While the equipment was clean, it was obviously old. All of it.

"I need to expand—we've got the demand for a larger place—but right now, I'm not sure how much longer I can keep going with this equipment. I'm afraid it's all going to break down at once, and if that happens, I'm out of luck. I'll have to close," Emily ended softly.

MJ murmured sympathetically. The host was a prima donna in real life, but Alex appreciated that she could turn on the charm when necessary. "What would that mean? If you closed?"

"It would impact way more than me," Emily said. "I've got a staff of twenty—they'd have to find other jobs. Most of them have been with me since we opened thirteen years ago. And the farms... for some of them, we're their biggest customer. It would be devastating. I can't, I simply can't allow any more farms to fail because of me."

Alex wanted to reach through the screen and hug her friend. She knew how deeply responsible Emily felt for those families who'd lost their farms after the lawsuit. Alex also knew Emily's own parents had sold their farm to a corporation after holding out as long as they could. Emily believed that's what killed her dad. He died not long after the farm changed hands.

"Tell us about your food, Emily. What makes you a good chef?"

Emily's face beamed. She loved cooking, the creativity, the intricacies, and the skill involved. It delighted her to learn a new technique, whether with a knife or with creating buttery, flaky layers in pastries. Alex had been the lucky taste tester for that whole experiment, and thought the extra miles on the lakeshore path were totally worth it. Emily explained her passion for inviting others to experience a complexity of flavors. She listed the farmers she worked with on her menu and her website. She considered eating akin to worship, and wanted her patrons to experience the same sense of wonder she did that something as simple as pulling a plant out of the ground, or off a tree, and preparing it well, could transport a person. Food had the power to elevate moods. Emily felt like good food and the joy it was capable of bringing could change the world.

"Running a restaurant is one of the hardest things in the world, but when I look around the dining room and see people connecting, truly connecting, over dishes I've created, it's the most gratifying feeling I've ever experienced," she finished.

Alex could see why Emily had been one of the four chefs selected out of thousands of applicants. Of course, she'd never had any doubt. She knew Em deserved it.

The interview wrapped up and the screen faded to black. There was a moment of silence before MJ looked up from her phone.

She slid it into the back pocket of her skinny black silk pants and lifted the microphone. "Now that's what I'd call a woman with a purpose, am I right?" she said, smiling automatically. "If you'll all take a seat, we can sample some of Chef Emily's, and our other competitors', creations. Each of the four chefs will create a different course every night. By the end of the fourth dinner, they'll have each cooked a four-course meal. After seeing tonight's menu, I don't envy our judges."

Dixon, who'd moved to stand next to MJ, took the microphone. "It's a tough job, but somebody's gotta do it," he said. The intimate crowd politely laughed.

Alex and William followed the group from the terrace inside. The large floor-to-ceiling glass doors remained open and the two sat at one of the small bistro tables scattered around the event space.

"Wonder if Emily feels like the Wizard back there," William mused, tilting his head at the row of curtains hiding the chef stations from the judges.

"Nah, she creates real magic," Alex answered, watching as Emily helped the servers load up their trays with the first course.

"Emily made the first course? Good. She can sit back and relax now," William said.

"Relax? If I know Emily, she'll jump in to help the other three. That woman's got more energy than a toddler at a candy buffet," Alex said.

A young man wearing standard server garb of white pressed shirt, black tie, and black pants placed Emily's appetizer in front of them. A white ceramic spoon with a curved handle sat on a black oval dish. They waited until everyone in the room was served and MJ spoke into the mic. "As you know, while it's not required, we invited our chefs to look towards what's available regionally for inspiration. Our first course definitely took that to heart: blackened trout topped with a cantaloupe salsa. I heard our chef personally picked the cantaloupe from Rocky Ford and even used local honey in the relish. Enjoy!"

William took a bite of the hors d'oeuvre and rolled his eyes back in pleasure. "O.M.G. That is amazing."

"It sure is. I love how the melon cools down the spice. And I bet that's white balsamic vinegar in that salsa."

"You've had this before."

Alex grinned. She knew this dish. Emily made something similar at her Chicago restaurant, using whitefish and mango instead of trout and cantaloupe. "Close enough. Remember, she made practically every meal for me when I was going through chemo." Alex's face suddenly flushed. She felt like her body was on fire; sweat dripped down her back. She removed her pashmina and draped it over the back of her chair. In the past few months she'd learned to always wear layers.

"Hot flash?" William asked. "Sorry. That has to suck."

"Yep. I can't believe every woman goes through this. It's debilitating," she complained, while dipping her napkin in her glass of sparkling water and dabbing the back of her neck. "Stupid drug I have to take for the next five years cuts off my estrogen. Menopause, here I am."

William grabbed the stiff paper with that night's menu printed on it and began fanning Alex. She smiled, then nodded to let him know she was better.

Conversation buzzed as servers cleared the first course and then, in succession, delivered salad and entree. LuEllen's salad was a bed of mixed greens topped artfully with hearts of palm, roasted red peppers, marinated artichokes, and tiny bay shrimp tossed with a Thai chili vinaigrette. The entree was grilled lamb chops, which Sergio had seasoned with garlic and cumin, and served with a wild mushroom risotto and a goat cheese and roasted peaches en croute.

There was a short break before dessert. Alex suddenly realized she hadn't used the bathroom the entire evening and that she had to go, and go now. She approached one of the servers. "Excuse me, but where is the ladies' room?"

He pointed down a hall that was painted a dark blue and instructed her to make two right turns. She did, following bronze sconces that provided dim light. After the second turn, she found a pair of all-gender bathrooms on the left. At the end she could see the main corridor. To her right was a swing door, a soft glow emanating from a small window. She was about to duck into the bathroom when she heard Emily's voice. *Uh oh*, Alex thought. *I know that tone. She is not a happy camper.*

Chapter 11

"What is this crap?" Emily shouted. Alex sidled towards the door and peeked in through the window.

Emily was facing the door. She held a large metal canister wrapped in white with black text on it. Alex recognized the generic label from her days working in a chain steakhouse.

"I'm not sure what you mean," Dixon said. Alex was surprised to see him in what was obviously a storeroom. *Maybe that's where he stashes his extra vodka*, she mused, then chided herself for the uncharitable thought.

"You know exactly what I mean," Emily spouted. "When you asked me to be on your little show, you promised you'd source all the ingredients from small farms, not this corporate BS."

The man sneered. "Seriously? You think we should buy flour? Panko? Sugar? From mom and pop running a farm stand?"

"Yes, I do, especially since that's what you promised."

"You're delusional. Typical chef. I promised no such thing. I said we'd focus on regional ingredients. I never said we'd buy everything from small producers.

Emily fumed and shook the canister at him. "You most certainly did. '*No corporate. Fair trade. Local whenever possible.*' That's what you said. I wouldn't have agreed to this if you hadn't."

"That's what Becca said; not me. And oh yes, you would have, Miss Kincaid. Remember? Your kitchen's falling apart. I'm your savior."

"Not at this price, you're not. I quit."

Dixon threw his head back, laughing. "Oh no you don't. You signed a contract. You walk off this show and I will sue you for everything you–don't–have. I will bury you in legal fees. Your ancient appliances will be the least of your worries." He stepped closer to Emily, inches from her face. Alex wanted to run in and rescue her friend. Instead, she stood in the hallway, gripping her fists so tight her nails dug into the palm of her hands. "I own you," he said, each word punctuated with a jab to Emily's sternum.

Mike, camera in hand, burst through the doors on the opposite side of the room that led to the back kitchen, followed closely by Becca and MJ. Alex could see the other chefs attempting to peer in, but Becca shooed them away. While the argument obviously could be heard in the kitchen, Alex hoped it hadn't carried all the way to the dining room.

"There you are!" Alex turned to see William at the end of the hall. She shook her head and put a finger to her lips to shush him, but it was too late. In her peripheral vision, she saw the crowd in the storeroom whip their heads towards the door.

"Fine," Alex heard Emily say. "I'll stay on your little show, but I refuse to use any of this trash." Emily walked towards a big black trash can and dropped the canister inside. The lid must have popped off, because a puff of white exploded like a mushroom cloud. Alex jumped back to avoid the swinging door as Emily pushed her way out of the storeroom. In the background, Dixon narrowed his eyes at Alex before smirking and turning back to the others.

Emily stalked down the hall, then turned around and flipped her middle finger in the direction of the swinging doors. "Em?" Alex said.

Emily shook her head, then stopped and her shoulders slumped. "You heard?"

Alex nodded. William looked from one friend to the other, but didn't say anything. "What are you going to do?" Alex asked.

"What choice do I have? It's only three more dinners, right? But I'll be damned if I'm going to use any of that corporate swill. I should have known."

"How? It's Dixon. They're supposed to be the best there is; you'd think they'd hold the same standards they do for their own products."

"I've been hearing rumors. *He*," Emily said derisively, "has been raiding the cookie jar so he can pay for another penthouse and upgrade his jet. Of course, I didn't hear a word of this until after I'd signed the agreement, and then it was too late."

"Hey, Alex? I hate to interrupt, but they're getting ready to serve dessert. Becca will have our hides if we're not there," William said.

Alex hugged Emily and held the embrace until she felt her friend relax. "Three more dinners, right? And I know you. You'll come up with incredible dishes, even if you have to go buy all the ingredients yourself." Emily nodded and Alex turned to follow William back to the dining room. Before closing the door, Alex turned to see Emily raise her head, straighten her spine, and walk back towards the storeroom.

Alex and William returned to their table. The room buzzed with conversation; it seemed none of the diners had heard the commotion between Dixon and Emily. Their desserts waited for them: raspberry puree drizzled over a flourless chocolate cake and topped with cinnamon whipped cream.

"Weird or not, Paul's got skills," William said.

Alex pushed back from the table and placed her napkin on her completely bare plate. "That. Was. Amazing."

"I could totally get used to this. My wardrobe, however, would hate me."

"We'll be working it off tomorrow. I heard we're climbing Seven Falls."

William was about to respond when MJ tapped a knife against her glass. The room's volume had increased with each course and each refill from the seemingly endless bottles of wine. It simmered to a whisper as the diners turned their attention to the host. Mike focused the camera on MJ and she smiled into the lens. "And there we have it. A delicious round of creations by our talented chefs. While the judges are sequestered and choosing their favorite courses, let's see yours by a show of hands." She listed the first course, and when the majority raised their arms for the appetizer, MJ laughed. "Well, there you go. A clear winner. Will the judges agree? We'll have to wait to find out."

William pushed back from their table and gave Alex his hand, helping her stand up. She put her arm through his and they followed the crowd out to the vehicles waiting to bring them back to their resort. "Oof," Alex said. "I can barely walk."

"That's why I only ate a small portion of each course," the woman behind her said, gloating.

Alex turned around. "Oh, hello Harriet. Well, good for you, I suppose. The bit of discomfort I'm feeling now was totally worth it." She rubbed her arms and stopped abruptly. Harriet crashed into her. "Sorry Harriet. I just realized I left my wrap inside. William, could you ask the driver to wait while I run back in?" She didn't wait for him to answer before turning and quickly walking back into the building. The young man who'd served them walked towards her, smiling, holding her pashmina in his extended hand.

"I believe this is yours?" he asked.

"Yes, thank you." Alex took it from him and remembered she'd never made it to the bathroom. She hurried past the show kitchen and turned down the hallway. As she neared the swinging doors that opened to the storeroom, Abbot came out and slid along the wall away from her and turned the corner. Alex released the breath she didn't realize she'd been holding, then entered the bathroom.

She went outside and boarded the shuttle. "Sorry, everyone," she said, lifting her pashmina. "I forgot my wrap and then had to go to the bathroom." She smiled at Emily as she passed her and found a seat at the back of the shuttle next to William.

"Is Emily okay?" he asked.

Alex shook her head and pointed her chin at the back of the seat in front of her where Harriet sat. The other woman had turned her head in an obvious attempt to eavesdrop. Alex didn't blame her. It was a hazard of being a journalist; every conversation could be material for a story. If Alex were still working for a newspaper instead of being a travel writer, what she'd learned about Dixon would have made for a great story. She knew the appliance company targeted chefs like Emily as their ideal clients. If word got out they were shortcutting the ingredients for their new signature show, it might not be devastating, but it would certainly impact their reputation with chefs who, like Emily, refused to compromise on quality. Although, from what Emily said, it sounded like Dixon raiding the cookie jar to fund his playboy lifestyle wasn't exactly news.

Chapter 12

"**N**o way. Uh-uh. Not going to happen."

Paul gave Harriet a playful shove. "What are you, scared?"

"Not scared. Smart. I mean, look. You can see right through those stairs."

"I'm sure they're perfectly safe. Thousands climb them every year."

"Exactly. That's a lot of weight to put on a few bolts holding a staircase to the side of a mountain." Harriet walked to a row of chairs and sat down, crossing her arms.

"Well, I'm going. You mean to tell me you're going to miss out on the view of all this?" Paul shouted after her, gesturing to the canyon. Alex put a hand on his arm.

"Let her be, Paul. This isn't something you can convince her to do," she said.

William agreed. "I'm certainly not afraid of heights, yet this gives even me pause."

Alex stared up the staircase. Halfway up, it turned so she couldn't see the final ascent from her current angle. Truth be told, she wasn't sure she'd be able to make it. They were at over 6,000 feet elevation and, as a lifelong Midwesterner, she was definitely not accustomed to the altitude. Add a steep climb to the mix and she knew it would be a challenge. She steeled herself. She beat cancer, damnit. There was no way she'd let her fear—or her body —keep her from this experience.

Harriet must have thought the same thing, because she appeared next to Alex with a look of resolve on her face.

"You don't have to do this, Harriet."

"Yes, I do. But I have to do it now."

"I'll be right behind you," William said.

They were at the base of Seven Falls, which was exactly what it sounded like. A cascade of seven distinct waterfalls began 181 feet above them. An enterprising soul back in the 1800s had turned the box canyon into a tourist attraction. The dramatic climb and ensuing views would make for a great segment for the show.

Alex and William walked towards the narrow staircase. After waiting for a stream of climbers to descend, she stepped on the first rung. She kept an eye on her feet; it was disorienting to see right through the open steps to the rocks. Her heart began racing. She slowed, putting her hands on both railings and using her arms to pull herself up. "Sorry I'm so slow," she said, apologizing to the line of people behind her.

"There's definitely no need to hurry on my account," Harriet puffed.

"Take your time," Mike said from behind William. He slowly panned his video camera up the falls. "I'm getting great footage."

Alex smiled gratefully, then resumed climbing. By the time she reached the landing at the halfway point, she needed to sit for a moment. So did Harriet, whose face had turned an alarming shade of red.

"You okay there, Harriet?" William asked, sitting next to her on the bench farthest away from the edge.

Harriet gulped and nodded. "Just need to catch my breath," she wheezed. Alex handed the woman her bottle of water as she walked over to the railing and looked down. Harriet sipped and handed it back. "Thanks, Alexis—um, Alex. Sorry," she said, having the grace to look sheepish. When they'd seen each other in Wisconsin, Alex had finally let Harriet know exactly how she felt about her habit of consistently calling her the wrong name.

"No problem."

William turned to Alex. "Ready?" When she grimaced, yet nodded, he took her hand again. "You're doing great. I'll turn you into a mountain woman yet." The two resumed their climb, and while Alex was again out of breath when they reached the top, William seemed completely unfazed. Even though the staircase was sturdy, the sheer number of steps was intimidating.

"Did you talk to Emily last night?" William asked as they began to climb back down. Harriet had elected to stay on the landing and Mike was shooting footage from the narrow creek before it plunged down the side of the mountain, so it was just the two of them.

"No. Sort of. I texted her to see if she was ok. She was, and she'd already found a source for her ingredients for today. All the chefs are checking out a farmers market and co-op this morning."

"What I don't get is how they wouldn't have known they were using corporate stuff. Didn't she get that out of the storeroom herself?"

Alex shook her head. "They put things like flour, sugar, etc., in canisters at their stations."

"Got it.

They reached the landing and stopped. William sat down next to Harriet and Alex again looked over the edge. At the base of the falls, standing next to the pool, she saw Becca and MJ standing toe-to-toe. Mike stood a foot away, and while his back was to them while he ostensibly shot footage of the cascading water, Alex had a feeling he was listening intently. This was confirmed when Becca's arms flung out, nearly knocking the camera out of his hands. Mike gave up any pretense of filming and stared at the two women.

"Hey William, come look at this," Alex said, motioning her friend over to the railing.

"Ooh. Drama."

"Let's head down. Seems like there's trouble in River City."

"I wonder where Dixon is?" William asked.

"Probably nursing a hangover. Did you see how he was slamming those drinks last night?" Harriet said from her corner on the landing.

"Perk of being the boss, I guess; unlimited supply of energy drinks and vodka," Alex shuddered. Harriet asked her how she knew what he was drinking. "The smell. I used to pour dozens of those a night when I bartended. I'd go home smelling like cigar smoke and Monster. Don't know which was worse."

They began descending the stairs, William in front of Harriet and Alex behind her.

"You need to climb up to the landing, now, MJ. It's in your script and it needs to happen," Becca said, so loudly they could hear every word even though they were still several steps away from the bottom. Becca gestured emphatically with tense, outstretched hands.

MJ looked down at her high-heeled sandals. "Fine, but if I fall, you'll have to deal with Dixon."

"I've been dealing with him all my life," Becca muttered to the departing host's back.

MJ pushed past William. Harriet gripped the railing, even though they only had a few more feet to go. Alex noticed Mike's eyes were focused on MJ's behind as she climbed. He looked away and caught Alex watching him. He shrugged. "See? Problem child," he said under his breath. Alex laughed, but sobered as soon as she faced Becca. Thunder played across the producer's face as she pulled out her phone and dialed.

"Where. Is. He?" Becca said before the person on the other line could answer. Although the sound was muffled, Alex distinctly heard "I don't know, Ms. Dixon. Nobody's seen him all morning."

Becca looked up, moving several feet away after realizing three journalists stood in earshot of her conversation. William narrowed his eyes at Alex. "Seems like we may have another mystery, Ms. Paige. Where oh where is the elusive Eric Dixon. Misogynist playboy, erstwhile appliance heir, and miserly misanthrope that he is, I suspect our dear Harriet here is right and he's suffering the consequences of his indulgence last night."

Alex shook her head. "You do get quite eloquent when there's drama afoot. Shall I start calling you Mr. Nathaniel Hawthorne?"

William gasped in mock horror. "That blowhard? Oh, forefend! You wound me."

"You two are ridiculous," Harriet said, then gestured towards the path away from the falls. "Becca's motioning for us. Looks like it's time to go." The three writers headed towards the shuttle. Behind them, Alex could hear MJ's shoes thumping on the metal stairs.

Chapter 13

The shuttle arrived at the showroom a little early. While William sat at a bistro table to reply to comments on his campervan's Facebook page, Alex studied the chefs' stations. She could tell which one was Emily's because her knife roll sat in the middle. Her friend's name swooped in big, fuchsia script across the black case. Emily's knives were custom-made. It was one of the few indulgences she allowed herself, although as she'd explained earlier that afternoon, it wasn't an indulgence at all. Her knives were the tools of her trade.

It had been enlightening interviewing one of her best friends. It was the first time in all the years they'd known each other they'd sat down as interviewer and subject. Alex knew the answers to most of her questions because of their long history, but it was the phrasing, the passionate articulation lighting Emily from within that gave her new insight. By the time they were done, Alex was even more convinced that her friend was put on this earth to connect people through food.

Paul was another story. From what she'd experienced of his cooking, she could tell he was talented, but it wasn't what drove him. The whole conversation was like peeling an overripe mango. Just when she thought she'd gotten a nice slice, the knife would slip and she'd be left with mush. While the other chefs had been transparent in their naked ambition and driving passions, Paul was opaque. Had he experienced some kind of childhood trauma? She simply couldn't get to the reason he wanted to be a chef in the first place, and why winning was important to him, if it even was. He said he wanted to win, but did he, really? She wondered.

Alex opened the cabinet behind Emily's station. Her curiosity was what made her a good investigative reporter and an even better travel writer. Some might call it snooping, but Alex called it a tool of her trade. She wanted to understand everything.

Inside the cupboard were shelves of plateware, extras of each item that sat on display in the glass fronted cases that lined the wall above the cabinets. There were small plates, large plates, and those black oval chargers Emily had used for her appetizer the night before. Presentation was part of the experience, and Dixon Kitchens made sure the chefs could create the effect they desired.

She began to close the cabinet when she heard a raised voice from behind the swinging doors that led to the kitchen.

"What? You gonna send me to my room?" That was definitely Dixon. Alex moved closer so she could hear better and peered through the window. She saw Becca leaning against the stainless steel island on one hand. Dixon leered at his half-sister with bloodshot, droopy eyes.

"Yes. You cannot be seen like this," Becca said. "Too many people will be here tonight."

"You can't make me."

"Want to bet?" Becca said. "You go out there in this state and I will pull the plug on the whole thing."

Dixon chortled. "You would not. You want this show just as bad as I do."

"I want this show *more* than you, which is why I will not allow you to ruin it. You've already done enough damage."

"You've already done enough damage," Dixon mocked. "God, you sound just like your mother."

"I'll take that as a compliment."

"What, no dig about my mom? I practically handed it to you on a plate."

Alex stifled a sneeze. The dry mountain air was really getting to her. Becca's head whipped towards the doors. Alex managed to move her head away from the window just in time. Emily rushed past her and pushed through the door, and Alex followed right behind her as if she'd just walked down the hall towards the kitchen. "Hi Becca," Emily said brightly. "I wanted to get this chard in some water. Look," she said, opening her tote and pulling out a bunch of healthy looking leaves. "Aren't they gorgeous? That farmers market was divine."

Becca's eyes snapped between the greens and Alex, who gave Emily a playful punch on the shoulder. "Put those away. I'm not supposed to see what you're cooking ahead of time."

"Oops!" Emily giggled. Alex almost rolled her eyes. Emily was not someone who giggled. "Silly me. At least you're not judging." She turned to Becca. "Did you know Alex is the reason I'm here?" When Becca raised her eyebrows, Emily continued. "I was going to throw the invitation in the trash, but she said I should go for it."

That wasn't true in the slightest, but Alex knew Emily was trying to cover for her eavesdropping.

Dixon popped open an energy drink and poured some into his rocks glass. He'd added so much vodka there wasn't room for more than a splash. He picked up the glass and tilted it at Alex, sloshing liquid onto the floor. "So it's your fault she's here, huh?" he slurred, capping it off with a wink.

Becca gripped Dixon's elbow. "And the show's better for it. Come on, Eric, I want to talk to you about some details for tonight." They turned to walk out of the kitchen, but not before Dixon leaned over and whispered in Alex's face. "I'm on to you," he said, extending his index finger without letting go of his glass and jabbing it between Alex and Emily. Becca propelled him through the swinging doors and turned him towards what Alex assumed were the offices.

"I'm onto you," Alex repeated, pointing her finger at Emily, who laughed, a full-throated guffaw. "That's more like it. I don't think I've ever heard you giggle before."

Emily shrugged. "I can play vapid when necessary. Don't like it, but I can do it. Figured it would get rid of them faster, and cover up your snooping."

"And I thank you for that. It seems I'm a little rusty when it comes to being stealthy," Alex said. "I'm a little surprised you can pull it off after last night. You were pretty livid."

"Still am," Emily said as she dampened a white towel and wrapped it around the stems of swiss chard. "I'm not happy about it in the slightest, but what am I going to do? I won't use that cheap crap, but I can't afford to walk off in a huff. I need that kitchen, and I'm determined to get it."

Alex assessed her friend. "Can't be easy."

"Not in the slightest. I feel sick that I've already used some of that junk, but now that I know, I can just bring my own." Emily pulled a kraft paper bag out of her tote. When she set it down, a cloud of dust floated up, and Alex figured it was flour to replace what Dixon had put in the canisters. She looked up as the doors swung in. "Hey, Paul. You want any of this for tonight? I got more of that double-aught than I needed at the co-op."

"I'm fine, thanks," Paul said. "Hey, Emily? I wanted to apologize for yesterday with Sergio. I don't know what came over me."

"Sure you do," Emily said. "You can't stand Sergio; he can't stand you; and the two of you are like a couple of bulls charging towards the same matador." Paul's chin dropped and Alex covered her mouth to hide her grin. Classic Emily. "As long as you keep that crap away from my station, you can go after each other all you want."

"Thanks for the permission, your highness," Sergio said as he plowed into the kitchen, nearly hitting Alex with the swinging door. "Sorry. Didn't see you there."

"No problem. Just trying to be a fly on the wall."

"This is a kitchen. We don't want flies," Sergio sneered, then joined Paul and Emily at the island and began unloading two bags stuffed with groceries.

"Watch it, Sergio. That's Alex, and if you're rude to her, I will put arsenic in your tea," Emily said.

Sergio threw up his hands in mock surrender, then turned and bowed with an exaggerated flourish. "My sincere regrets, m'lady. It wasn't my intention to offend."

"Are you related to William, by any chance?" Alex asked. Sergio squinted and then turned his head to Emily, who'd burst out in another full-throated laugh. "Looks like you three have your hands full, so I'll leave you to it," Alex said and rubbed her hands together. "Can't wait for dinner!" She turned to leave and nearly caromed into LuEllen. The grandmotherly woman let out a stream of curses and Alex was suddenly glad LuEllen didn't have knitting needles in her bag. Those could be deadly.

Realizing she had an audience, LuEllen plastered her trademark sweet smile on her face and changed her demeanor entirely. "Oh dear. I am so sorry. What a silly old fool I am, bustling around and not paying any attention. Are you alright, my dear? Can I get you anything? A cup of tea?"

Alex thought of Emily's threat about the arsenic, and after the sweet old woman's outburst, decided she should back away and leave these lovely, volatile people to themselves. "No, no, I'm fine. It's my fault. Really. I need to get back out there before they kick me out for keeping you all from creating another amazing meal." Alex turned and mouthed, "You OK?" to Emily, then turned when her friend dipped her chin.

Chapter 14

A lex dabbed the corner of her mouth and set her napkin on the table. She pushed her chair out and followed William, and everyone else, outside. In the distance, the red rocks glowed like flames, and real fire danced atop rectangular stone tables. Alex headed towards the rattan couch closest to the open doors, setting her wine glass on an end table. William sat next to her, and Harriet took one of the chairs.

Dixon bustled towards a stage set in the corner of the terrace. He must have taken a nap because Alex hadn't seen him throughout the dinner and he seemed a little less indisposed. He grabbed a microphone. "What a dinner; am I right? Those chefs are on fire, aren't they?" He took a drink while waiting for the group to respond appropriately. When they murmured, he continued. "They're not the only thing that's on fire," he said, then gestured towards the showroom. A trio of performers carrying batons walked through the doors, and as they passed Alex and William, each lighted the ends. Alex could smell the fuel as the flames took hold. The three split up. The band kicked into *Earth, Wind and Fire*. Dixon spoke again. "I present Alchemy." He put the microphone back in the stand and walked away from the stage, draining his drink as he went. He rounded the corner and approached Becca, who was standing behind Alex and William. "I need another drink," Alex heard Dixon say to his half-sister. "Want one? Oh, that's right. You never drink when you're on the job."

"One of us has to remain sober," Becca said.

"I am sober," Dixon whined. Alex could practically see him pouting.

"Right. You keep telling yourself that," Becca said. William dug his fingers into Alex's thigh and she knew he was hearing the siblings, too. Alex still couldn't quite grasp that those two were related.

Alex turned around and saw Dixon enter the showroom. Becca glared after him, then she turned to face the view. She crossed her arms and drummed her right fingers aggressively on her left bicep. Alex could feel her anger reaching towards her like the fires dancing from the tips of the batons.

"You're staring," William said.

"Ugh. I'm still doing that, aren't I?" Alex had spent so much time alone, she sometimes felt like she'd forgotten how to be around people.

"Staring's fine. We just need to work on your subtlety. Watch me, for example."

Alex focused on her friend. His face was directed towards the band in the corner, but she could see he'd focused elsewhere. She followed his gaze to the other side of the terrace where Sergio sat with his eyes closed and his head resting on the back of the couch. Paul approached and stood in front of him. Sergio opened his eyes, and although Alex couldn't hear him over the band and the snapping flames, she could see him sigh. He slowly picked his head up and looked at Paul. Even though he was seated and the other chef stood over him, Sergio still seemed dominant.

"Wonder what's going on with those two?" Harriet asked, startling Alex. Harriet had been so uncharacteristically quiet Alex had forgotten she was sitting right there.

"Could it be? No. Looks like Paul's extending an olive branch," William said. Indeed, Paul reached his hand towards Sergio and held it there, waiting. After several beats, Sergio clasped Paul's hand and the two shook. Paul waved his arm to the empty portion of the couch and, when Sergio gave him a slight nod, sat down next to him.

"Interesting," Alex said. "Who would have th–" A scream pierced the air. The band stopped and the fire dancers froze. "That's Emily." Alex jumped off the couch and raced inside. She could see Emily through the open doors to the back kitchen. As she raced towards her friend, she nearly collided with Abbot, who was racing away from the kitchens. He dropped his rocks glass and it shattered on the marble floor. "Watch it!" he shouted, then doubled over, his face a motley shade of green. Alex leapt out of his way, narrowly avoiding his projectile vomit. She crashed into William and stumbled, but he caught her and they ran together. "Em! Are you okay? What happened?" Alex skidded to a stop and William slammed into her back. She teetered, but managed to keep her balance as she looked at the body of Eric Dixon, face down, one of Emily's signature knives sticking out of his back.

Emily turned. Her face was ashen. Alex and William stood on either side of her and led her away from the body towards a chair in the corner. Becca entered the room and braked as soon as she saw her brother. She grabbed the radio from her belt. "Mike," she called. "I need you in the back kitchen now. Tell everyone to stay where they are."

Another scream cut her off. MJ stood in the doorway, her hands covering her mouth. "No no no! No! It can't be! Not my Dixon!" MJ tried to push her way past Becca, who stopped her, gripping her by the shoulders. MJ continued to scream hysterically. Becca slapped her.

"I bet she's been wanting to do that for a loooong time," William said. Alex shushed him.

"MJ," Becca said, her voice low but stern. "Pull yourself together."

MJ abruptly stopped her shrieking and glared at Becca. "You did this, didn't you? You've been jealous of him your whole life. He told me all about it. Are you happy now? You killed the love of my life!"

Alex noticed MJ's cheeks were completely dry.

Becca rolled her eyes. "Stop the dramatics, Marjorie. He was no more the love of your life than he was my favorite brother."

"He's your only brother, you heartless—"

"Half-brother, thank you, and while I'd never choose to be related to him, I'd also never murder him."

"Are we sure he's dead?" William asked timidly.

"Are you daft?" Sergio said. He stood in the doorway; behind him Alex could see LuEllen trying to peek over his shoulder but she was too short. Stellar stood behind her. Harriet and the other journalists crowded around trying to get a glimpse. "Seriously, man. It's obvious."

Jo tapped Sergio on the shoulder. "Excuse me, please. I have some experience with situations like this."

"What? Like, you've killed people?" MJ shrieked. Becca rolled her eyes again.

Jo ignored MJ. She entered the room and spied a box of gloves on the counter. After snapping them on, Jo circled Dixon's body, avoiding the pool of blood that was slowly congealing. Jo knelt down and felt for a pulse. "He's dead. Becca? I assume you're notifying the authorities?"

Becca had her phone to her ear and nodded. "You've got this?" she asked Jo. When she nodded, Becca walked towards the swinging doors that led to the storage room at the other end of the kitchen. She stopped before walking through and leaned against the wall. Despite her bravado, Alex could see the woman was upset.

Jo stood up, straightening the creases in her pantsuit. "While we wait for the authorities to arrive, I suggest we all go into the showroom and get comfortable. None of us is going anywhere for a while, I'm afraid."

"I'm not leaving him," MJ said. "He was my everything."

"Stop the histrionics and get out there." Becca hung up and pointed. MJ glared, but did as she was told, following the crowd of onlookers reluctantly making their way into the showroom. Emily started to get up from the chair, but Becca stopped her. "Ms. Kincaid, I think you need to stay right where you are." She didn't say *Until the police arrive*, but they all knew that's what she meant.

Emily nodded and put her face in her hands. Alex rubbed her back and shook her head when William looked at her. "That's my knife," Emily said. "How did it end up...that's my knife."

Chapter 15

“D on't say another word, and definitely don't say anything to the police.”

Emily whipped her head up to stare at William. “You don't think I did this, do you?”

“What? No way, Ms. K. Not in a million years. Remember, I'm dating a cop. I know how it works.”

“He's right. We know you had nothing to do with this, but it's best to keep quiet and let them investigate. Whenever they get here.” Alex looked at her watch. The response time seemed fairly slow for a murder.

The front door slammed open. “Where is it?” a deep voice growled. “Take me to the body.” For his voice to carry from the front door to the back kitchen meant he must have been shouting. Anger crossed Becca's face and she pushed open the swinging doors, walking through the storeroom towards the front of the house. The muffled voices grew louder and clearer as they approached. “In here? Fine. Go sit with the others.” A police officer pushed his way into the kitchen, banging the doors against the shelves on either side. Three more officers followed him, the one directly after him catching the swinging doors before they could slam into her. The first officer saw Emily, Alex, and William in the corner and stopped. "What are those three doing here? Get them into the other room with everyone else."

"Officer...Thompson?" Becca said, reading his name from the tag on his uniform. "I'm Rebecca Dixon. The seated woman is here because she found the body."

"Detective Thompson," he corrected. "And the other two?"

"Ms. Kincaid's had a shock. They're here to support her."

"And you? Why are you here?"

"Someone had to stay with him, and since this is my business and my show, it's me."

The officer raised his eyebrows. "Your business? I thought it was his."

Becca sighed with frustration. "I don't think right now is the time to get into who owned what."

"I'll decide that," Thompson said, but he let it go. "You three," he pointed to William, Emily, and Alex. "Get out there with the others." He followed them into the show kitchen. "Quiet!" he shouted. Every head in the room turned towards his bellow. "I'm Detective David Thompson of the Colorado Springs Police Department. Eric Dixon has been found dead. You are all required to stay here until we are done interviewing each and every one of you. Is that clear?" All but one murmured acquiescence.

"What? No!" Abbot shouted. "It's obvious what happened. I saw that pink-haired nutjob standing right over him with blood on her hands."

"That's a lie!" Alex said. "There isn't a speck of blood on her."

"Then you admit she was standing over him, and it was her knife in Dixon's back?"

"Stop right now. You," Thompson said, pointing to Abbot. "Follow the officer. We'll talk to you first."

Abbot turned and smirked at Alex before following a uniformed woman. "That rat bas—" Alex started. William put his finger on her lips. "Fine. I won't say it. But what you want to bet he's the murderer and he's trying to pin it on Emily."

"You—Ms. Kincaid, is it? You come with me."

Emily hadn't even had a chance to sit down. She turned to William and Alex and nodded her head. "I'll be fine," she said, glancing between them and lightly squeezing their hands. "I heard you." She gave them each a significant look and Alex knew her friend would follow William's advice to be quiet.

"Enough. Get over here," Thompson said to Emily, then spoke to his two male colleagues waiting by the open doors to the back kitchen. "You two stand watch until the crime scene techs arrive. You," Thompson said, pointing to the closest officer. "Stay right there and make sure everyone stays in this room. Is that clear?" Thompson glared at the young man, then shifted to sweep the room. He waited for Emily. When she neared, he grabbed her by the arm and took her down the hall.

Emily yanked away from his grip and continued walking, her head held high. "Good for you, Em," Alex whispered.

"What a tottering swag-bellied canker-blossom," William said.

"Power-hungry egomaniacal misogynist is more like it." Alex drummed her fingers on the table. "Emily's smart. She won't say anything."

"You know what has to happen now, don't you?" William asked.

"What?"

"Don't play innocent with me. You're already assessing everyone here to figure out who killed him."

"Who, me?"

"Nice try, but we both know there's no way you're going to let Barney Fife in there take Emily's fate in his hands. She'd swing from the gallows before breakfast if it were up to him, especially with Mr. Misanthrope pointing the finger at her."

Alex continued to stare at the hallway where Emily and the police officer had disappeared, then she turned her gaze to William. "I don't have a choice."

"No, Ms. Poirot. You don't. I can already see those little gray cells buzzing."

"Will you be my Captain Hastings?"

"Certainly, although I do hope you'll be a bit kinder to me than a certain detective was to his trusty sidekick."

"But of course."

Harriet flopped into the empty chair at their table. "I think next time I'm invited on a press trip I'll find out if you two'll be on it so I can refuse," she said, glaring at them.

"What are you talking about, Harriet?"

"Two trips in a row. Two murders." Harriet pointed back and forth between the other writers. "I think you attract drama."

William laughed. "Yes, because we're the reason an obnoxious man who didn't seem to rub anybody the right away—except MJ—was literally stabbed in the back. From what we'd already seen, seemed like a rather fitting end."

"William Meriwether Blake. No one deserves to be murdered."

"I can think of a few," he muttered. "Anyway, did you see anything, Harriet?"

"No. I was outside with you, remember?"

"Yes, but you had a different angle. We were facing the mountains. Your chair was turned, so I thought maybe you might have seen someone slip in or out of the showroom."

Harriet waved her hand dismissively. "I wasn't paying attention. I was watching the fire dancers."

Alex closed her eyes, trying to recreate the scene on the terrace. It was a blur. She punched her thigh with her closed fist in frustration.

"What's wrong?" William asked.

"Stupid chemo brain," she said, then waved her hands around her head. "I know the information is in here, I just can't get to it."

"That's still an issue? Hasn't it been months since you had chemo?" Harriet asked incredulously.

Alex glared. Harriet, of all people, should have known better. But then Alex remembered that Harriet's mom was still undergoing chemo when she'd died of breast cancer, so there was no way Harriet could know how long recovery could take. Alex softened her gaze. "Yes, but it's the gift that keeps on giving, just like this blasted radiation rash." She flipped her hand. "It'll come to me later. William, what do you remember?"

"I'm afraid I won't be much help, either," he said. "I was too busy enjoying the scenery."

"And by scenery, you mean Mike?"

"Yes, and also Sergio, and that divine bass player. He's as tasty as dinner was."

"Ugh," Harriet said in disgust. "Aren't you dating that Door County cop? What would he think of your flagrant ogling?"

"*Flagrant ogling*," William repeated. "I like that. No, really, I do! Don't worry, my dear. Billy gets me. My eyes may roam, but my heart stays true."

Alex laughed. "You're such a romantic. Back to what you remember, OK? Anything at all?"

William frowned. "Let's see. Mike was shooting the fire dancers and the band. I think MJ was leaning against the wall. Yes, she had her phone out and looked bored as all get-out. That woman obviously has no appreciation for the finer things in life." He stood up and reached for Alex's hand. "Let's go outside. If I see it, I might remember more."

Alex took William's hand and he helped her up. They began to walk towards the terrace. "Hey! You there. Where do you think you're going?" shouted the officer assigned to keep everyone in the room.

William turned around. "My friend here needs some air. It's been quite a shock. We'll just be out here. It's not like we can go anywhere."

The officer looked down the hall, then turned to Becca. "Are there stairs out there?"

"No," she said. "The only access is through the showroom."

"Officer–what's your name, sir?" Stellar asked.

"Franklin," he said.

"Officer Franklin, while I know you're doing your job, and it's in all our best interests to make that easy for you, we've all ex-perienced something extremely traumatic. A little understand-ing would go a long way," Stellar said, her voice soothing. Alex imagined that's how the chef dealt with entitled customers at her restaurant. Being in D.C., she would have had lots of practice.

"Fine. But nobody leaves until Detective Thompson says so, got it?"

Alex and William nodded and resumed walking. The rest of the room seemed to collectively sit back in their chairs, including the waitstaff that had gathered at the booth where Abbot had been sitting. The glass doors to the terrace remained open and Alex walked through first. She pulled her pashmina close to ward off the slight chill in the air. She could still smell the fuel from the fire dancer's batons as she waited for William. He'd gotten caught behind the band, who had been leaning against the floor-to-ceiling windows but moved towards the terrace as soon as Officer Franklin gave the go-ahead. They walked quickly to the corner where they'd left their instruments during the chaos surrounding the discovery of Dixon's body, followed by the fire dancers and William. He sat on the same couch in the same position he'd been in before their evening was so rudely interrupted by a murder.

William closed his eyes. "Yes, that's right. MJ was over there," he pointed towards the north wall of the terrace. "She was standing next to that door. Wait, there's a door?" He briefly opened his eyes. "I didn't even notice that before. Except, apparently, I did. Anyway, she was over there. Mike started filming from behind that couch and worked his way past MJ towards the fire dancers." William shook his head. "That's all I remember. Your turn?"

Alex followed William's example, closing her eyes and breathing deeply. She sighed, frustrated. "All I can see is those spinning batons. And Sergio and Paul. It seemed like they were arguing again, but then Paul sat down next to Sergio, so I assumed they worked through whatever it was." She rattled her head. "That's it. That's all I've got." Alex moved her feet as Harriet stepped in front of her and sat down in the chair she'd occupied earlier. "What do you remember, Harriet?"

"I told you. Nothing."

"Just try, okay? For Emily's sake."

Harriet exhaled. "Fine. Let's see. I think Stellar and Jo were sitting on that couch. I remember thinking how completely opposite they were. I don't remember seeing LuEllen or Abbot, though."

"Abbot was coming out of the kitchen when I ran in to see what had happened to Emily," Alex remembered. How could she have forgotten that? The man nearly puked on her. She clenched her hands into fists, tired of fighting her mind. Before chemo, she could recall events with rapid-fire accuracy. Now she sometimes felt like she'd forget her own name. Once, during treatment, she was talking with her nurse and he'd asked what her diagnosis was. She couldn't remember.

She couldn't remember. The diagnosis that had upended her life, and she couldn't remember.

Alex took a deep breath and closed her eyes again. She felt William's hand cover hers and they intertwined their fingers. Her heart rate slowed.

"It's coming back. Paul stood in front of Sergio, then sat down next to him. Jo and Stellar were kitty-corner to those two. The other writers all sat on those two couches." As she pictured it, she realized that all the writers had segregated themselves to one side of the terrace and the chefs and judges to the other. That was unusual; often there'd be an integration since the writers were there to cover the event. Maybe it's because they were all tired and full, and they'd already conducted several interviews that day. Alex knew she had simply wanted to sit, relax, and enjoy the show, the music, and the view.

"I'm surprised they sent a detective right away. Aren't they usually called later?" William asked.

"Not when you're a one-percenter," Harriet replied. "You know as well as I do they get special treatment."

"True. And I bet dollars to Deloreans Becca made sure to tell them exactly who and how important the victim was."

"Of course I did," Becca said. She put her hands on the back of the couch and leaned over, and William and Alex turned so they could see her better.

"What's going to happen with the show?" Alex asked, curious at how long Becca has been standing behind her.

"It'll go on, as they say. Detective Thompson wants everyone to stay in Colorado Springs. I told him that was the plan, although we do have an excursion to Royal Gorge planned tomorrow. He said as long as we all go, that's fine, but we 'better not lose anyone.'" She snorted.

"So we're going to just act like nothing happened?" Harriet asked. "Isn't he—wasn't he your brother?"

"Half-brother. And yes. What happened is unfortunate, but Eric was more the face and figurehead. He did little if any real work and had no idea what goes on behind the scenes, so his death will have little to no impact beyond the inconvenience of this investigation. And the fact that someone here killed him."

"Yeah, there's that tiny wrinkle," William said wryly. "Who do you think did it?"

"Not Emily," Becca said, to Alex's relief. "That woman wouldn't hurt a fly."

"See? Told you," Alex said. "She literally won't hurt flies. The woman's fierce, but she's a pacifist and believes all life is sacred. Emily would never, ever kill someone."

"Especially with her own knife. Did you see how protective she is of those blades? She'd never sully one with something so pedestrian as murder." William tapped his forefinger on his cheek. "So then, who had motive? Who would have wanted him dead?"

Becca tossed her head back and laughed, startling everyone else on the terrace. She covered her mouth, shaking her head. "Everyone who ever met him, including me."

With that, Becca turned away and walked towards the west wall of the terrace. The full moon lit up the snow-covered tips of the mountains like the edges of a giant saw blade.

Alex reached into her bag and pulled out her pen and journal. She began writing and was soon lost in the words appearing on the page. She barely noticed when William set a cup of coffee on the table next to her.

Chapter 16

"Where were you when you heard Ms. Kincaid scream?"

Alex sighed. This was the third time Detective Thompson had asked her to go over the evening's events, but she knew better than to remind him with a snide comment like *As I said...* "I was outside, sitting on the couch closest to the showroom. William sat to my right. I was facing the band and the fire dancers had just begun performing. Harriet sat in a chair to my left."

"As I've told you before, Ms. Paige, I am not asking you where everyone else was. I'm asking where you were."

Since she already answered him, she didn't respond.

"What happened when you heard Ms. Kincaid scream?"

She told him again about running through the showroom. Abbot nearly vomiting on her. Seeing Dixon's body. Emily standing in shock. She recounted the rush of the other people all clamoring to see what happened, and how Jo and Becca took control.

"Jo, that's Mr. Primrose?"

"Ms. Primrose," Alex corrected. What an insufferable neanderthal, Alex thought. *I bet he's got a pickup truck with a cab full of empty beer cans. No, stop that,* she told herself. *He's just doing his job, and part of that includes getting witnesses riled up. His misanthropic behavior is probably all an act. Yeah, I'll go with that.*

Detective Thompson flicked his wrist. "Whatever. With a name like Primrose, it's no wonder," he muttered. He looked up at the other detective standing in the corner of the office. It was the first time since Alex had been in the room that he acknowledged the other woman. "Sally, take her back and then bring me, let's see," he consulted his notes, "William Blake. Go," he said, turning from his partner to his notes without looking at Alex.

"Yes, sir," the woman said.

Alex peered at her nametag as they entered the hallway. "Detective Miller?"

"Yes?"

"How in the world can you work with him?"

The woman, who appeared to be in her mid-thirties, stopped and turned to Alex. "Ms. Paige, if this is some misguided attempt to connect with me because we're both women, it's not going to work." She extended her arm, inviting Alex to walk in front of her.

Maybe I'm losing my touch, Alex thought, then shook it off. She'd been watching the female detective while Thompson repeated his questions, and she knew she'd caught a few looks of disdain and at least one eyeroll. She'd just have to be more subtle if she wanted to get under her professional armor. Alex knew Thompson was simply going through the motions; he'd decided Emily was the killer and he'd shoehorn her in even if it was painful. She needed an ally. "I'm sorry, Detective Miller. That was rude of me."

The detective nodded, but continued her purposeful stride and they were soon standing next to William. "Mr. Blake? Come with me, please."

William searched Alex's face, squeezed Emily's hand, then stood up gracefully. "My pleasure, Detective. The sooner we can get to the bottom of this, the better." He turned to wink at Alex and let the detective lead him towards the hall.

Emily's knee bounced up and down like a jackhammer. Alex was tempted to put her hand on her friend's leg to quell the shaking, but decided it would be better to let her expend her energy. "How was it? What did he ask you?" Emily asked.

"What you'd expect. Where were you, what did you hear, why did your friend kill Mr. Dixon." Emily guffawed and her leg stilled. Alex had known if she said something so absurd it would have that affect on her.

"It's ridiculous. Like I'd use my own knife to stab someone and then stand there screaming like an obnoxious horror movie starlet. Seriously. Do I look that stupid?"

"Sadly, because you're a woman, to that neanderthal I'm afraid you do. I honestly can't believe he's got a female partner. He must have been forced into it."

"I saw you talking with her. How is she?"

"A pro. I need to tread carefully with her if I want to get her to confide in me."

Emily sighed, sat back, and tilted her head to the ceiling. "I'm sorry," she said.

"For what?" Alex replied, shocked.

"Your first trip back after cancer and you had to deal with a murder, and were almost murdered yourself. Now there's another one. I'm sure this isn't how you imagined your grand return would be."

Alex leaned over and took Emily's hands. She waited for her friend to look at her. "Listen to me," she said. "This is not your fault. You didn't hear what Becca said, but she told William and me that pretty much anyone who ever met Dixon wanted to kill him. Not exactly a resounding endorsement, and it creates a pretty big suspect pool. You are the least likely person to do this, especially, as you said, with your own knife. Whoever chose that as a weapon was just sloppy."

"Unless you're Detective Dumble-Dumb in there. I wouldn't be surprised if he arrested me tonight."

"He is *not* going to arrest you. I won't let that happen."

Emily gave her a small smile. "Do you have any ideas about who did it?"

"I'm working on it. Question for you: Abbot came racing out of the kitchen. Was he in there when you found the body?"

"No," Emily said, shaking her head. "I went to the bathroom, then went to the kitchen to put the rest of my ingredients in the refrigerator and I wasn't paying attention. I walked behind the island and there he—the body—was. Then I saw movement at the entrance to the room—that must have been Abbot coming in—but it didn't register." Emily gulped and lowered her head. "Then I screamed. Abbot came towards me, looked at me, looked down, and then he raced out. Oh, god, it looks like I did it, doesn't it? He's right; I was standing right over him and it's my knife and they're going to arrest me but I didn't do it, you know I didn't." Her voice rose with her panic level.

"Of course I know you didn't. Don't be ridiculous."

Emily calmed down. "Thank you."

The friends sat silently. William returned and reported Thompson had asked him the same questions he'd asked Alex. "He kept calling Jo *him*," he said. "Neanderthal."

One by one, Detective Miller shuttled people back and forth to be questioned. The longer the evening dragged, the louder everyone got. People traded looks of suspicion, many of them directed at Emily. Abbot repeatedly walked up to the officer guarding the back kitchen, looking at his watch and gesturing. Each time, the officer pointed him to the showroom. Abbot would walk to his table in the corner, glaring at Emily. Finally, after about an hour of this, he walked directly to their table. "This is your fault," he hissed. "You did this. Why don't you go confess and let us all get out of here."

Emily refused to respond, just stared him down.

"Fine. Consider your restaurant dead, because even if they don't arrest you, I will ruin you."

Emily didn't move. Sergio suddenly appeared behind Abbot. He leaned down and spoke into his ear. "I wouldn't make threats, if I were you."

Abbot's head whipped around and he stumbled backwards. Sergio glared. Abbot scrambled off to his corner, stealing glances at the angry tattooed chef before focusing on his empty rocks glass. William got up to pull out a chair for Sergio, grinning the whole time. "You, sir, are magnificent. I'd certainly scurry away if you talked to me like that."

Sergio accepted the proffered chair. His eyes didn't leave Emily. "We've been talking," he said, nodding to LuEllen and Paul, who sat a couple tables away. "We know you didn't do it. No chef would ever use their own knife to kill someone."

"There's also the shocking idea that Emily wouldn't kill someone in the first place," Alex said defensively. Sergio treated her to one of his searing glares. She raised her hands. "Fine, fine. But I know you know Emily. The others may not, but you do."

"Sure do. And I told Detective Incompetent in there exactly that."

At that moment, both detectives entered the showroom. Thompson cleared his throat. "Everyone," he bellowed. "You are now free to leave. However, do not leave the area."

The room erupted. Becca approached the detectives. "May I?" she asked. He flipped his hand as if to say go ahead. She turned to face everyone. "I've spoken to each of you, but as a reminder, we will continue with this production." The room groaned. "It's what Eric would have wanted."

William stifled a laugh. "I guarantee that's for the police's sake," he whispered.

"Detective Thompson has graciously provided permission for us to continue as planned with our visit to Royal Gorge tomorrow since we're going as a group. Because we've all had an excessively late night, and a traumatic experience, we'll get a later start. I remind you that you each signed an NDA. That includes tonight."

"This is ridiculous," Abbot said, standing up and knocking his chair over. "We all know she's guilty. Why don't you just arrest her and be done with it?"

Detective Thompson narrowed his eyes at the food critic. "Mr. Abbot, I don't write about restaurants, so why don't you stop trying to do my job? I guarantee you wouldn't be very good."

Alex released the breath she hadn't realized she'd been holding, and heard Emily also exhale.

"You heard him," Becca said. "He's got a job to do, and so do we. The shuttles are waiting to take us back to the resort. Barring any arrests, I expect you to be in the lobby at ten. Waitstaff? Same time tomorrow as today. Or, I guess now it's same time today as yesterday."

They all stood up. Alex saw Harriet approaching her. "Who do you think did it?" Harriet asked.

"I don't know. I just know Emily didn't."

"What, your little exercise on the terrace didn't reveal the murderer?"

Alex stopped. "Harriet, I'm tired. We're all tired. Can we not do this right now? I'd like to get back to my room in peace, if that's not too much to ask."

Harriet huffed. "Fine," she said, and sped up to get in front of Alex. They all entered the shuttle. Abbot took the front row and stretched out so no one could sit next to him. *Not that anyone would want to*, Alex thought.

Chapter 17

Despite getting back to her room at two in the morning, Alex still woke up early. At home she never slept past seven and her body was still on Central time. While she loved the quiet of pre-dawn, she could have used a few more hours of rest. Instead, she got up, started the coffee maker, and opened the curtains. The sun was just beginning to rise, and rays glistened off a fresh blanket of snow, even though it was late September.

Alex opened the window to breathe in the brisk air, then sat at the desk with her coffee and journal. Her morning ritual had become even more important during her treatment. Not only did it help her process everything she'd been feeling and experiencing, writing helped her remember. She was afraid without it, she'd lose all memories of this time, and she wondered if she'd ever feel confident in her brain again.

She shook her head. She knew that was fatalistic and untrue. She'd already noticed her responses were coming quicker and she didn't struggle as much to make connections. The most frustrating part was knowing the thoughts were there, the words were there, swimming somewhere in her brain, but she just couldn't get to them. It was like they were always out of reach. For someone who'd always believed she was born to write, that miasma was terrifying.

Alex wiggled her pen back and forth like a seesaw, then began to write. She recorded everything she could remember from the previous two days, including sketching the terrace's layout and who was where. She realized a couple key players were missing, or maybe the timing was off a bit.

Today would be interesting. It didn't surprise her that Becca wanted to continue the plans to visit Royal Gorge. She had contracts to fill and commitments to meet. Plus, there was obviously no love lost between the half-siblings. While to some it might have seemed cold, Alex appreciated that Becca didn't try to fake mourning. In fact, Dixon's death probably made it easier on her. From everything she'd been hearing, the man had been more of a liability than an asset. He was abrasive, greedy, rude, and basically a total tottering swag-bellied canker-blossom, as William had so eloquently called him. Still, nobody deserved to die. Almost nobody. Alex could think of a couple people she'd investigated during her newspaper years that were irredeemable.

Alex rattled her head to shake the stained memories. *Sure, I can remember that clearly*, she thought ruefully. *Ask me what happened yesterday and forget about it.* She looked down at her journal and re-read her notes, and to her relief, realized she'd remembered more than she thought. An idea formed. She stood up and walked to the French doors. Snow melted off the evergreen boughs like a gentle rainstorm, disappearing as the rising sun warmed the air. By the time she left her room, it was as if the snow had never been there.

"I'll wait here."

"Harriet, c'mon. It's perfectly safe," Paul said. He put his hand on the back of her arm and began tugging her towards the bridge. Harriet dug her heels in, shaking her head vigorously. "The only way to beat your fears is to face them."

"Actually, that's not true," William said. He turned to Harriet and spoke gently. "You don't have to go if you don't want to."

"Doesn't she have to? Isn't that why you're here? What kind of journalist are you?" Paul scoffed.

Alex glared at him. The more she was around the California chef, the more she distrusted him. Underneath, she suspected there was something darker. "Paul, why is it so important to you that Harriet confront heights?"

"Because it would be a shame for her to miss out on this," he said. His words held good intentions; his tone did not.

Sergio walked up to stand beside Harriet. "I suggest you take your hands off her. If she wants to cross the bridge, she will, but not because you've forced her to *face her fears* or some such nonsense. Seriously, man. Can't you see you're embarrassing her?"

Harriet wrenched her arm away from Paul. "All of you; leave me alone." She stalked off in a huff. While Harriet always huffed, Alex thought this time it was completely warranted.

"If you change your mind…" Paul called after her, then grinned before turning towards the line to take a tram across the gorge.

"What an insufferable ass," LuEllen said. She walked over to Harriet, and this time her demeanor reflected her grandmotherly appearance. She called Sergio over, and the two talked with the short reporter. The three came back to where Alex and William stood, Harriet in between the two chefs. "Harriet's going to walk with us across the bridge. We're going to stay on either side of her and protect her."

Alex glanced towards Paul, who was talking with Abbot. The two turned their eyes towards her, and she swore their faces were filled with malevolence. Why would they have that much anger against her? She didn't even know them. Then she realized they weren't looking at her, but just beyond. She turned around to see Emily approaching. Alex looked between the two angry men and her friend. The men turned around to face the front of the line. *What was that all about?* Alex wondered, then shook herself off.

"Want us to go with you?" William asked.

"No, please. No. This is embarrassing enough as it is."

"Miss Raven," William said sternly. "There is absolutely nothing to be embarrassed about, do you hear me?"

Harriet nodded.

"Good. Looks like you're in good hands. We'll just saunter casually behind you three and take in the view," he said, wiggling his eyebrows at Sergio.

Harriet laughed, then smiled gratefully at William before walking slowly between LuEllen and Sergio towards the highest bridge in North America. Alex heard a drone fly overhead and turned to see Mike piloting the aerial camera. Emily was walking back towards the park's entrance, passing Mike, her phone to her ear. She turned to face Alex and made a stabbing motion, then grimaced as she realized what she'd done. She smiled sheepishly, shrugged her shoulders, and kept walking towards the tables outside the visitor center.

"It feels wrong, doesn't it?" William asked.

"Being here?"

"Yes. A man was murdered last night, and no matter how foul he may have been, you'd think there'd be some kind of, I don't know, mourning period."

Alex agreed. "What's sad is that not a single person seems to be terribly torn up about this, except for maybe MJ."

William scoffed. "Miss Crocodile Tears? I think she's more concerned about losing her sugar daddy."

"That is quite a cynical take on that young woman's grief."

"Appearance of grief, you mean. I know you've noticed she hasn't shed a single tear, no matter what her words say." William walked to the side of the bridge and looked down into the gorge. "Whoa. That's a loooong way down."

Alex joined him at the railing. "You know they used to have an elevator that would take you down to the river? Now that would be a cool ride."

"What happened to it?" William asked. Alex knew he'd driven Bessie, his camper van, out to Colorado Springs and hadn't had time to do his customary research.

"It burned, along with almost everything that was here. There was a huge fire in 2013. Pretty amazing they only lost a few planks on the bridge."

"Double-whoa," he said. He turned to face Alex, leaning his elbow on the railing. "So, Ms. Holmes, who do you think did it? Who did Dixon in?"

Alex continued to watch the river. From almost a thousand feet above, it seemed to flow languidly between the canyon walls, even though she could see froth indicating its pace was much livelier. "I honestly have no idea. I know Emily didn't do it—"

"Naturally."

"—and Sergio was sitting on the terrace the whole time."

"Are you sure? You seemed to question that last night."

Alex nodded. "I'm sure. I wrote everything I could remember this morning, and I could distinctly picture Sergio walking outside in front of us. He turned right and sat a little closer to the stage, and we turned left. I remember because I was watching you, and you were watching him. Did you even see any of the fire dancers?" she teased, nudging her friend in his side.

"Of course I did. I saw a flame or two." William turned to watch the tram crossing the gorge. "There go Paul and Abbot. Now those two seem like the kind to stab someone in the back."

"Paul? Really? I could see Abbot, but Paul? I don't know. He seems more passive aggressive than that. Like he'd think it, but never actually do it."

"I know what you're saying, but there's some anger there."

"Probably not as much as Abbot has. That man has serious serial killer vibes."

"Why Alex Paige. That seems a bit harsh, especially coming from your PollyAnna mouth."

Alex shuddered. "The man is vile. But, even if Paul was angry enough, I don't know. A knife seems too messy for him. Too violent." Her eyes flickered. "Have you noticed he puts on gloves the minute he gets into the showroom?"

"Which means no fingerprints. Hmmm."

The tram approached the station at the other end of the gorge. Alex pushed back from the railing and began walking. She saw Harriet, LuEllen, and Sergio take the last step off the bridge onto solid ground. The two chefs raised their arms; Alex could hear them shouting in celebration and watched as they hugged Harriet.

"Those two definitely didn't do it," William said. "What about Becca?"

"Maybe," Alex said. "I couldn't place her on the terrace. Last I saw, she'd been leaning against the windows. She's certainly got motive."

"And with Emily's knives sitting there like an invitation, she definitely had means. Oh! Look! There's a zipline!" William picked up his pace. "I'm surprised she left them out."

"They had to leave their knives at their stations. Dixon 'commanded' them to get out on the terrace with everyone else. I could tell Em definitely wasn't happy about it. She kept looking back into the showroom." Alex paused. "I wonder. Maybe she saw something? I'll have to ask her."

William looked around. "Where is she, anyway? Wasn't she just with us?"

"On the phone," Alex said, pointing across the bridge. They could see Emily's fuchsia hair in front of the visitor center. "There's a local sales rep and she's trying to get her knife replaced before tonight. It probably won't have her signature handle, but she'll make do."

They reached the end of the bridge and William made a beeline for the zipline. "We are SO doing this," he said, grabbing Alex's hand.

"Of course we are," she replied. "But first don't you think we should see what else is over here? We don't have all day."

"Nah. We'll take the zipline, then ride the tram back. That way we get to do it all. Besides, screaming our fool heads off will be good for us."

Alex laughed. William was irrepressible. It was one of the things she loved most about him. As they neared the ticket booth, they passed Abbot. William called out to him, but the critic ignored him. "I agree with you about the serial killer vibes. That man is ice, if ice were hatred wrapped up in a tiny package with a bad combover." They reached the counter and William turned his attention to the attendant. "Two, please. My treat," he said, turning to Alex.

"You know the show will pay for that," Harriet said from behind.

William shrugged. "Probably, but this wasn't on the agenda, and I need to do it because my editors will eat it up."

Harriet shuddered. "You're going, too, Alex? You sure you should be taking risks like that? I mean, after what you've been through."

The matronly tone irritated her, but Alex knew the other woman meant well. "That's precisely why I'm doing it. You never know what's going to happen."

"Well, hope you make it. I'm going to ride the carousel. The nice, slow carousel." Harriet walked towards the brightly-colored merry-go-round. Alex and William strapped in to the zipline and flew across the ravine, screaming, as William had said they should, their fool heads off.

Chapter 18

"Detective Thompson, this is ridiculous," Becca said coldly. "Look what you people have done." She gestured to the canisters on the floor. Several had popped open, spilling beans, flour, and what looked like quinoa in piles of various colors and textures. "These ingredients are ruined. How are we supposed to run a cooking show without ingredients?"

"You aren't. This is a murder investigation, Ms. Dixon. I would think you'd want to know who killed your brother."

"Half-brother," she corrected. "He was stabbed. What are you doing in here?"

"The Coroner found evidence of ethylene glycol in his system," answered Detective Miller.

"Miller. What did I tell you about staying quiet?" Thompson reprimanded. Detective Miller blanched, but Alex could see her defiance as she lowered her head. She might be displaying acquiescence, but there was more going on beneath her servile attitude.

"He was poisoned?" Becca asked.

Thompson glared at his colleague before answering. "Looks like it. So this," he said, gesturing to the mess in the storeroom, "is us doing our job."

"And keeping me from doing mine."

The policeman chortled. "You really think you're going to shoot tonight? Fool. This is still an active crime scene."

Becca simmered. She looked up and saw Alex and William standing in the corner with Emily. She focused on the chef. "Emily, please get Sergio, Paul, and LuEllen and meet me in the office. You two," she said, pointing at William and Alex, "get Mike. Tell him where I'll be. NOW."

They filed out of the storeroom, Emily turning to talk to the other chefs, who were all waiting in the back kitchen. Alex and William continued through the kitchen into the showroom and found Mike talking with his assistant. "Becca wants to see you in her office," Alex said. "Apparently someone also tried to poison Dixon and now the police are saying she can't do the show tonight."

Mike's eyes rounded, then he smiled. "Oh, we'll still do the show tonight. I guarantee it."

He walked towards the hall and Becca's office. William watched him. "I know Becca's determined and forceful, but you saw that disaster. There's no way they're going to shoot here tonight, even if the cops let them in," he said.

"All they need is a big enough kitchen and lots of ingredients. I wouldn't be surprised if she weren't already calling someone."

A few minutes later, Becca proved Alex right. She came down the hall, the chefs behind her like a row of toddlers heading to the playground with their nanny. "Folks, change of plans. Who here's been wanting to try *Mio Salumi*?" She nodded at their approval. "We're in luck. They're graciously opening their kitchen to us tonight so we can continue the show uninterrupted," she said, then muttered under her breath, "despite Detective Thompson's interference." Becca straightened her shoulders. "Right. Chefs, get what you need. Mike's gathered some tubs you can use for your things and a van will be out front. The rest of you, come with me."

Alex marveled at the woman's efficiency. Becca had been in the background while her brother, er, half-brother, had been around, but now she seemed to come entirely into her own. She was a force to be reckoned with, and without Dixon's obvious ineptness, Alex knew Becca would take the company to even greater heights.

Talk about a motive.

William placed his napkin on his empty plate and patted his flat stomach. "Divine. Simply divine," he said.

Alex agreed. Becca had turned the calamity of being kicked out of the showroom into an opportunity. She asked the four competing chefs to create a new, Italian-themed menu, which would be served not only to the judges and journalists, but also to any of *Mio Salumi*'s diners, if they wanted it. Most of them did, and that meant the chefs were serving dozens instead of a handful. Alex could see Emily's fuchsia hair bobbing around from station to station in the restaurant's open kitchen. Occasionally, Em would make eye contact with her and grin. She was in her element. So were Sergio and LuEllen. Alex couldn't hear the older woman, but she could see her lips were sealed and had a feeling LuEllen was humming. *Just like grandma*, Alex thought, and decided then and there that the older woman did not kill Dixon. "Anyone who hums when they're cooking is not a killer," Alex said out loud.

William followed Alex's gaze. "Mrs. Sweet Home Alabama over there? Agreed. She definitely wouldn't murder anyone. Maybe a 'gator, but then she'd skin it, filet it, and you'd have a new purse and a plate full of kebabs."

Alex laughed. "Speaking of... those jackfruit kebabs were outstanding. Fantastic way to start the meal."

"Say what you want about Paul. He may be a jerk, but he can cook. And what about Emily's entrée? Man oh man."

"Divine," Alex said, echoing William's earlier comment. I love how she played on Sergio's antipasto. That gnocchi with gran padana and capocollo was so simple, so elegant—"

"And so delicious," Becca said.

Alex looked up and saw the reflection in the windows of the producer standing behind her. She turned to face her. "I don't know how you pulled this off."

Becca shrugged. "Chef Mario and I go way back. He owed me a favor, and they were able to shuffle some of the reservations to make room for us."

"Nice they had the private banquet room available for the judges," William said.

The producer nodded. "I knew it would work out. So, we have one more day of exploring tomorrow and then our big dinner and reveal at Garden of the Gods. You ready?"

"So soon?" William asked. "Any hints on who's the winning chef?"

Becca wagged her index finger back and forth. "Now now, you know I can't tell you that. Besides, they're all winners." Her eyes sparkled, surprising Alex. "I better go check on LuEllen. Her dessert should have been out by now."

Alex watched Becca walk to the kitchen. "What are you thinking?" William asked her. "The disco ball that is your brain is blinding me."

"She really wants them all to win," Alex said with wonder. "Did you see her? She was practically glowing. You know, I'm beginning to see why Stellar is so loyal to her."

"Still think she could have killed her brother?"

"Half-brother. I honestly don't know."

"The poison aspect is a new twist. What do you want to bet they put the, what was it, ethylene glycol in his drinks?"

Alex agreed. "I Googled it. I knew it was antifreeze, but I didn't realize it could make someone seem drunk."

"Perfect poison for Dixon, then."

"Yep, and somebody could pour it into his vodka and energy drink abominations and he'd never know," Alex said.

William shuddered. "Slip a dose into his bottle of Belvedere and bam."

"But then why was he stabbed? Do you think two people tried to kill him? Or did somebody get impatient?"

Before William could answer, a server slid the final course in front of him. He burst out laughing, and Alex joined him. "Oh, LuEllen, you are brilliant," he said. The Alabama chef had created a dessert of raspberry mousse topped with peach sherbet shaped like a crustacean. It looked almost exactly like shrimp cocktail.

"Enough talk about death and murder. This looks amazing." After taking a few photos of the creative dish, Alex took a bite, smiled, and turned towards the kitchen, catching LuEllen's eyes. Alex raised her hands to clap and mouthed, "Brava," to which the chef dipped her head in a shallow curtsy.

Chapter 19

William leaned back in the barstool and groaned. "I am still full."

"You and me both," Alex agreed. She took a sip of her white crème de menthe, the chilled liqueur instantly settling her stomach. Since her audience considered food one of the main components of travel, she was used to eating richly while traveling; however, this week had been excessive. No wonder, with four of the best chefs in the country competing for a new kitchen.

William leaned over the bar to address Emily, who was seated on Alex's other side around the corner of the bar. "Why does Abbot have it out for you so badly?"

Emily shrugged. Sergio, seated next to her and facing William, spoke up. "Because he can't get to her," he said, in his gruff baritone. "He tried reviewing *Elements* once, but Em here knew who he was and refused to serve him. 'We've got enough scathing reviewers in Chicago; we don't need you,' she said. The man sat there for three hours and couldn't even get a glass of water." Sergio laughed. "Classic Emily."

"Why was he in Chicago in the first place?" Alex asked.

"James Beard Awards," Emily said. "Abbot's been trying to go national for years, and, from what I can guess, he figured lambasting restaurants in the city where the awards were taking place was the way to do it."

Alex shook her head. "It's amazing he sat there for that long. He doesn't strike me as the patient type."

"He's a snake," Emily said. "He thought he could get to me, get to my people, but nope. If I'm going to get a bad review, it'll be because I've earned it, not because of some fool who tries to make a name off of ruining people. No matter what we gave him, he'd find something wrong with it. So we gave him nothing. All publicity is good publicity, my ass."

"And he didn't write about you snubbing him?" William asked, causing Sergio to laugh again.

"This one here," Sergio said, pointing his thumb at Emily, "called Abbot's editor and told him what she'd done, and that if she ever saw a review about her restaurant with his byline, she'd sue his pants off. Abbot's column took a sabbatical for a few months after that."

William looked at Emily in awe. She sipped her martini. "You, my fine fuchsia flocked friend, are magnificent," he said.

Alex grinned, then sobered. "She is. However, he's certainly trying to make you pay for it," she said to Emily.

"He can try."

"He is. And Detective Thompson seems happy to oblige. Abbot's local. I wonder if the two know each other?"

"Sure do. Thompson got Abbot out of a few DUIs," Becca said from behind Alex, startling her, again.

How does she do that, Alex wondered. *The woman's as stealthy as a lynx.*

"Hmmm," Alex murmured. She turned to Becca. "Any word about the poisoning? Did they find the antifreeze?"

"Yes," Becca answered. "In the storeroom. It had been poured into a flour canister. One of those big metal ones."

Alex gasped, turning to Emily, whose face had turned the color of double-ought. "We need to figure out who did this, and fast," Alex said.

Becca looked back and forth at Alex and Emily. "Why? Oh. I remember. You and Dixon had that slight disagreement about his choice of ingredients."

Emily put her elbows on the bar and sunk her head into her hands. "Nothing slight about it," she said, her voice muffled.

"It sounds like someone's trying to frame Em by putting the poison in one of those canisters," Alex said.

"You know, I could totally see Abbot doing that," William said. "But did he know about the argument? He was in the dining room, wasn't he?"

"Oh, he heard about it. Abbot—" Becca stopped, then rattled her head before continuing, "—is a critic. He pays attention. OK, then. I've got an early day tomorrow." The producer accepted a shot glass from the bartender, slammed back the liquid, grimaced, and wiped the corners of her mouth. She put the glass back on the bar and spoke to Emily and Sergio. "And you two have a very, very big day. I'll see you in the morning."

Alex watched her walk off. "That's not what she was going to say about Abbot."

"No, it wasn't," Mike said, turning to face them. He'd been sitting with his back to them at a high top. None of them had noticed he was there. He leaned in conspiratorially. "I heard the day after their little confrontation Dixon tried to bribe Abbot to make sure Emily lost."

"What?" Emily shouted. "That snake. They're both snakes. They're all snakes."

"You're insulting snakes," Sergio said calmly.

"Fine. They're, they're," Emily sputtered, "they're reprehensible."

"And one of them is dead," Mike pointed out, "and someone's trying to make it look like you did it."

Emily slammed her first on the bar, startling the other patrons. The bartender approached. "Miss? Is there anything I can do for you?"

"No, no. I'm sorry. I'm fine. It won't happen again." She raised her gray eyes to Alex. "What am I going to do?"

Alex reached over and hugged her. "You're going to cook. You're going to make a brilliant dinner tomorrow and you're going to win your new kitchen. You are going to do what you were put on this earth to do." She patted her friend's back and pulled back. "I've got this, OK?" Alex asked. Emily nodded and sniffed. Sergio casually passed her a bev nap.

"I've also got an early morning," Alex said while getting up from her barstool.

"You always have an early morning, Miss Morningdale," William interrupted.

"True, and this time, so do you."

William groaned. "Really? Fine. I'll acquiesce to your tortuous hours, but I better not hear a word about the impact it has on this lovely visage." He waved his hand in a circle in front of his face with a flourish. "Miss Em, only for you, my dear. Only for you." He pushed back, walked over to peck Emily on the cheek, then winked with one eye at Sergio and the other at Mike. "Come

come, Ms. Holmes. I need to get as much beauty rest as I can before we begin our day of sleuthing."

Alex squeezed Emily tight, moving to the side so Mike could take her seat at the bar. She looked at the two men. "You two take care of her. I don't think she should be left alone." They nodded, and Alex turned to follow William into the lobby.

"Do you really think Emily's in danger?" William asked as they walked over the arched bridge.

"I don't want to take any chances," Alex replied. "Whoever killed Dixon used her knife and stored the poison in a container with which she's associated."

"Now I know you're serious."

"How?"

"You always use precise grammar and never, ever end a sentence in a preposition when you're serious."

Alex nodded grimly. "Dead serious." She blanched. "Oh gawd, that was awful. Yes, we're going to find out who did this and convince Detective Thompson." They reached their neighboring rooms. Alex touched her keycard to the plate on the door, turning the handle when the light switched to green. "I'll get you at seven."

"With coffee. A large, no, make that a giant coffee."

"It's like you don't even know me," Alex said with a weary smile, then closed the door behind her.

Alex grinned at the thin layer of blue goop covering William's face. "So that's your secret, eh?"

He frowned and opened the door wider so Alex could enter. "Do you think my pristine skin happens naturally? Well, it did, but it's a lot of work to keep it that way. A lot of work that takes time, you know, and early mornings do not allow enough time."

Alex thrust a giant steel-walled tumbler at him. "Here. This will help."

"Savior!" he shouted, gripping the cup with both hands. "Give me two shakes and I'll be right with you." William entered the bathroom. Alex leaned against the doorframe and watched as he wiped the moisturizing mask from around his lips, took a sip of his coffee, and sighed. He then set the cup on the counter and finished cleaning the goop from his face. After a splash of cold water, a few dabs with a plush white towel, and another sip, he joined Alex. "I'm as ready as I'll ever be. Shall we?"

They crossed the bridge over the lagoon and entered the main building of the resort. Alex steered them towards an intimate library. She sat down on a leather couch tucked into an alcove beneath shelves of books, curling her legs under her. William sat across from her in a wingback chair. "I feel the distinct need for a smoking jacket," he said.

"We'll check the gift shop later. First, let's go over what we know." Alex pulled a spiral-bound notebook out of her cross-body bag and flipped to a section she'd flagged with a sticky note. She glanced over her notes and sketches, then handed the notebook to William so he could review what she'd written.

"Looks pretty thorough. Not that I'd expect anything less. So what's the plan?" he asked, handing the notebook back to her. "Why am I up at this ungodly hour?"

"I thought we'd go through the suspects one-by-one. You know the drill: we're looking for means, motive, and opportunity. We also need to figure out who had all three, but also had alibis."

"Or we know couldn't do it, like Emily," William said, then took another sip of his coffee. "Delightful. Hazelnut?"

Alex nodded absently, turning back to the first page and running her finger down her notes. "OK, then. Suspects. We've got Becca."

"Definite motive." William crossed his leg. "Shouldn't we start by ruling out Emily?"

"I think that's harder to prove. We know she's innocent, but with the way she's being framed, I think we need to rule other suspects in."

"OK. So, Becca. I hate to say this about two fine examples of my gender, but Mike and Sergio are also suspects."

Alex flipped to a blank page, jotted the three names down the left side, then wrote "M, Mo, Opp" along the top of the page, creating columns. "Let's name them all and then we'll fill out the rest," she said. "Abbot and Paul, obviously."

"Definitely," he said. "What about LuEllen? And don't forget Stellar."

"Or Jo."

William gasped. "Not Jo! Fine. Write her down."

"Of course, there's our favorite reality show host, MJ," Alex said, writing the two initials.

"Ah yes, Miss Crocodile Tears. An actor that one is not. Is that everyone?" William asked.

Alex scanned the list of names. "Yes. Well, except for Emily, but since we know she didn't do it, we're not even going to include her. That would be bad juju."

"Bad juju indeed. Alrighty then, shall we start at the top?"

"Becca. She's got motive," Alex said, putting an X under the Mo column. "She's got the means, too," adding another X.

"Everybody had means, since the knife was sitting out there plain as day."

"True, but I'm thinking about the poison, too. They've got a garage at the showroom, and I bet there's antifreeze there."

"So we've decided that one person poisoned him and stabbed him?"

Alex leaned back and looked up, momentarily blinded by the lights under the shelving above her. She lowered her head and blinked to clear the spots from her vision. "I guess not. I suppose it could have been two different people. Although that seems awfully coincidental. Maybe we should assume it was one person for now."

William gave her a small frown. "You're really worried about Emily, aren't you?"

"Yes, but why do you say that? Beyond the obvious."

"Because you're never one to assume anything."

Alex huffed, exasperated. "Yes. Fine. You're right. But we don't have much time. We have to be at the shuttles by nine and it's already," she consulted her watch, "seven-thirty. I just want something solid to go on."

"So you can interrogate the suspects, muah ha ha," William said, drumming his fingers together.

"Darn right. Now Becca. She probably had access to antifreeze. We know everyone had access to the knife. Opportunity?"

William shook his head. "I don't know. I only saw her briefly. She was leaning against the windows before I turned around to watch the dancers."

"Watch Sergio, you mean," Alex said, putting a question mark in the Opp column for Becca. "Speaking of, what possible motive could he have had?"

"That Dixon was an ass?"

"Yes, yes, but to try to frame Emily? It seems to me he's got something else in mind when it comes to her."

"Maybe that's why," William said. "She doesn't reciprocate his feelings. Frankly, it seems like she's pretty oblivious to what's obvious."

"Obvious to you," Alex said. "You're the romantic. I just don't see Sergio killing someone. Someone who didn't deserve it, I mean" she corrected, remembering that Sergio had, in fact, killed someone.

"Which doesn't exclude him, since Dixon definitely deserved it." He raised his hands at Alex's glare. "I'm just saying. The man seemed to have no redeeming qualities." William yawned. "Let's keep going or I'm going to fall asleep. OK. Sergio does have a temper. Dixon could have said something to make him really, really angry. He could have grabbed the closest knife, followed Dixon into the back kitchen, and stabbed him."

Alex marked X's under M and Mo. "But wasn't he on the terrace when Dixon was stabbed?"

"I think so, but we don't know for sure when it happened. We only know it was sometime after Dixon told everyone to go outside."

"That wasn't much time." Alex snapped her fingers and pointed at William. "He couldn't have done it. We followed him outside, remember?"

William grinned, with a slightly lascivious tilt. "Oh yes, I remember."

"And that was right after Dixon told us all to get out there. And since you were watching him practically the whole time…"

"Can you blame me?"

Alex marked a line through Sergio's name.

"What about the poison?"

"One thing at a time," she said. "We skipped Mike. What about him?"

They continued going through each name. By the time they met the others in the lobby, Alex felt like they had a pretty good idea of who killed Dixon based on means and opportunity. The one thing she didn't have is motive, and that's what she aimed to find out. She just hoped she had enough time to change Detective Thompson's mind. If he arrested Emily before the evening's final competition, it would be disastrous. Beyond the whole suspicion of murder, if Emily couldn't compete she'd end up losing her restaurant.

Alex was not about to let that happen.

Chapter 20

It was a short drive to Cheyenne Mountain Zoo. Everybody, except Harriet, was waiting in the lobby when Alex and William joined them. Alex immediately went to Emily and hugged her tight, then squeezed her hands. Emily squeezed back. "Thanks," she said. The two boarded the bus, followed by William, and walked towards the back. Emily peeled off to sit across the aisle from Sergio. Alex was beginning to see the two had more of a connection than she'd realized.

The shuttle was about to take off when Harriet came bounding in. She settled into the row behind Paul, who turned around. "Hey Harriet, I didn't get a chance to ask you: how was the bridge?" Paul asked.

Sergio, sitting a few rows up, spoke up without turning around. "Stop being an ass," he growled.

Paul glared, then broke into a benign-looking smile. "I'm merely asking her if she enjoyed it, since I noticed you and grandma ever-so-kindly helped her across."

"Go ahead," LuEllen said sternly. "Please, I insist. Go ahead and call me 'grandma' again."

"Like you don't want people to call you that. I mean, look at you."

LuEllen laughed, dispelling the tension. "Gotcha!"

Paul glared at her this time, then masked his anger with another mild smile. The shuttle lurched to a stop, ending the exchange, but Alex noticed Paul continued to focus on LuEllen.

They exited the shuttle. The sun shone brightly. The snow from the previous morning was long gone and Alex was glad she'd checked the weather before leaving her room. The temperature looked to be about thirty degrees higher than the day before. She stretched her arms, welcoming the warmth.

"What in the world is he doing," Abbot asked, pointing at Jo, who stood by the entrance to the zoo and spoke while facing her phone.

"She," William corrected, mid-yawn. "She's shooting a video. What's it look like she's doing?"

"It looks like *He* is making an ass of *him*self," Abbot shot back.

"Only one person doing that," William said, looking pointedly at the critic.

"Children," Becca said. She watched Jo and waited until she was done with her video. "Jo? Can you join us? Good. They've graciously opened the zoo early for us. Tonight's the big finale so you chefs need to be back with plenty of time. Good news: Detective Thompson has released the showroom. I've asked our staff to make sure everything's ready to go so you can prep.

"Writers and judges," Becca continued, "you're free to explore as you like. Chefs, stick with Mike. We want to make sure we get footage of you feeding the giraffes. He's got some other shots he hopes to get, too, right?" Mike nodded. "Ok then. Meet back here at noon and then we've got one more stop before we return to the hotel to freshen up."

Becca turned and walked towards the entrance, where a young woman wearing a khaki uniform opened the gates.

Alex caught up with Emily, who was following the park employee with Mike and the other chefs. "Mind if we tag along?"

"Of course not," Emily said, then leaned to whisper in Alex's ear. "How's it going?"

Alex knew she meant her investigation. "We've narrowed it down to a few possibles," she whispered back. "Still too many for my liking, but I'll get it figured out."

"I know you will," Emily said. She nodded at Sergio. "We know he didn't do it."

"Yes, he was outside the whole time. This one can verify that," Alex said, poking William in his side.

"Can I ever."

"What about LuEllen?"

"Nope. She was sitting with Stellar and Jo from the time Dixon ordered us outside until you screamed." Alex blanched. "Sorry."

"Don't worry about it. So that rules out all the chefs but..." Emily tilted her head slightly towards Paul, who was walking ahead of them with his hands in his pockets.

Alex nodded. "There are others, though, including him," she said, indicating Mike. The videographer seemed unlikely, but she and William hadn't been able to pin down his movements.

They reached the giraffe pavilion and the park employee led them in. At Mike's direction, Emily joined the other chefs while the ranger gave them handfuls of romaine lettuce. One by one, they fed the animals. Emily laughed with sheer joy as the giant black tongue curled around the sheaf of green. LuEllen cooed to her giraffe, and even Sergio broke a smile. Paul held back.

"Go on, Paul," Sergio urged. "What are you, afraid of a little tongue?"

"Now who's being an ass," Paul mumbled. "There's nothing little about that thing. It's gross. It's disgusting. Here," he said, shoving his lettuce at Emily. "You feed it."

Mike captured the entire exchange, a slightly wicked smile on his face. "It's going to be mighty interesting to see what clips of Paul appear in the final production," William said. "Mike seems to like catching him in unflattering moments. Not that he has many flattering moments."

MJ climbed up the stairs and clomped across the wooden planks. "Becca said I need to feed this?"

Mike turned his camera towards her. "It's about time. Where were you?"

"The shuttle left without me, again. Becca needs to fire that driver."

"Or, you know, you could be on time," Mike replied, keeping the lens focused on her.

She flipped him the bird, then turned the full wattage of her on-screen personality to the ranger. "Hello, Karen," she said, reading the young woman's nametag. "Can you introduce me to your little friend?" MJ followed Karen to the giraffe and Mike dutifully recorded the show host's interaction with the stately animal.

William watched MJ and Mike. "I wonder," he mused.

"What's going on in there?" Alex wiggled her finger at his head.

"I may not have a disco ball for a brain like some people, but I've got a few bright spots. Hey! I got it! I'm a strobe light," William laughed, then whispered. "I think, now I may be wrong, but I think, just maybe, Mr. Mike there doth protest too much when it comes to Miss MJ."

Alex turned to watch the host and the cameraman. "Hmm. You know? You may be right. They've got that frenemies feel to them."

Paul called from his post several feet away from the giraffe and the other chefs. "What are you two rambling on about?"

"Just remarking on how cool it is we get this opportunity. How often do you get to feed a giraffe?" William said.

"Never, and that's fine with me," Paul replied. He returned his gaze to Emily, watching as she and Sergio alternated feeding their last leaves of lettuce to the animal. He checked his watch. "Are we about done here? We don't have all day, and didn't you have other things you wanted to see?"

Mike turned his camera towards Paul again. "Yes, your highness, as soon as MJ and I finish doing our jobs."

William gripped Alex's sleeve and pulled her towards the end of the platform. They leaned on the railing and looked out over the path that wound further into the zoo. "The plot thickens."

"Or Paul's just insufferable and Mike's tired of it. I don't blame him," Alex said.

Emily appeared on Alex's other side and looped her arm through hers, leading her towards the steps. "C'mon," Emily said. "Mike said we're going to see the lizards next." They clambered down the wooden risers to the path, followed closely by Sergio and LuEllen. Once they reached the asphalt, Alex turned around. Mike and MJ shared a small smile before the host flipped her hands dramatically. "Where are the hand wipes?" she demanded. "Becca told me you'd have hand wipes."

Mike pulled a packet out of the camera bag strapped around his waist. Before MJ could take one, Paul rushed in and grabbed the packet, yanking several wipes out of the plastic container. "Whoa!" Mike said.

Even though Paul had refused to feed the giraffes, he still aggressively wiped his hands as if an animal had wrapped its big tongue around them and drooled all over him. He visibly shuddered. "I apologize," he said to Mike. "I have a thing about animals. We don't get along." He sounded embarrassed, and Alex thought it was the most sincere thing she'd heard come out of his mouth since she'd met him.

"Shouldn't you face them, then? Isn't that what you told Harriet?" Sergio said.

Paul narrowed his eyes. "This is different."

"How so?"

"It just is." Paul stalked off. Alex noticed Sergio was grinning and Emily was shaking her head.

"You just love to get him riled up, don't you?" Emily said.

Sergio nodded. "It's so freaking easy. C'mon, Mike. Don't we have some lizards to see?" He turned to follow Paul. Emily walked beside him.

"I wouldn't be surprised if those two started holding hands," William said. "I think we have a little romance brewing."

"I certainly hope so," Mike said, his camera trained on the couple. "Makes for good TV when romance goes awry, and it always goes awry. MJ, why don't you tag along with them?"

MJ sped up slightly to catch up with the two chefs, squeezing in between them. She put her arm through Sergio's and focused entirely on him, ignoring Emily. Emily slowed down until she was next to Alex and William. "You going to let her get in on your man like that?" William teased.

"First of all, he's not 'my man.' Secondly, I give her five seconds before she stomps off in those ridiculous shoes," Emily said. William began counting, and before he reached *four*, MJ did as

Emily predicted. Mike sped up, and he and MJ entered the reptile enclosure with the ranger.

When they reached the pavilion, Alex turned around and saw LuEllen struggling. She waited for her. The zoo was named Cheyenne Mountain for a reason, and the elevation combined with the incline of the path made climbing difficult unless you were used to it. Coming from literal sea level, LuEllen was definitely not used to it.

"Thank you, my dear." LuEllen was breathing heavily. "How's the investigation going?" Alex raised her eyebrows. "You're not exactly subtle," LuEllen explained.

Alex nodded. "Former investigative reporter," she explained. "Old habits die hard."

"It's a good thing they do, or else that one's going to be in trouble," LuEllen said, pointing at Emily. "That detective sure seems to have a thing for her. He wouldn't believe it's anybody else even if he found fingerprints, DNA, and had a full confession."

"There's got to be a story behind that. I mean, it's not rational how focused he is on her."

"Sure it is," LuEllen said. "Emily found the body, poor thing."

"Ergo, she's the one who killed him," William said.

"Did not," Emily called, making them all laugh.

Mike and MJ returned with Ranger Karen, opening the door. "We've recorded MJ's bit and I've scouted out where you'll be," he said to the chefs. "MJ will tell you where to go. And Paul? No need to worry. These scary beasts are behind glass."

Sergio snickered as he fell in behind MJ. The rest of the group followed. Emily and Alex both raced to the windows. "They're adorable!" Alex cooed, as the lizard's long skinny tongue flicked.

"More tongues," said Paul. "Great."

"It's a theme," William said, sticking his out. "I will say, these creatures' linguas are much more impressive than ours. I'm going to have to work on that."

MJ tapped Alex on the shoulder. "You're in frame," she said.

Alex and William followed MJ so Mike could get his B-roll of the chefs, except for Paul, admiring the reptiles. LuEllen laughed. "You think those are lizards? You should come to Alabama, friends. I'll show you lizards."

"I suppose you've got alligator on your menu," Paul sneered.

"You're darn right I do. Gator gumbo, gator cocktail, gator jerky; I'm the veritable Bubba Gump of gator."

"I thought you were all about shrimp?"

"Do I strike you as one-dimensional, my boy?" LuEllen said.

"I'm not your boy," Paul muttered.

To their left, Sergio and Emily were sticking their tongues out at a blue monitor. Emily giggled, Alex noticed, then did a double-take. Emily was giggling? For real this time?

From his place between Alex and MJ against the wall, William crossed his arms. "Is it just me, or is Paul's sad little man act getting extremely boring?"

"It's not just you," MJ said. "Good thing Mike's good at what he does. He'll turn that crap into gold."

"Why, Miss MJ. I do believe that's the first nice thing I've heard you say about our captivating cameraman."

MJ blushed, ever so slightly, but enough for Alex to notice. "He is rather attractive, in that rugged outdoorsy kind of way, isn't he?" Alex asked, keeping her voice casual.

"Mm-hm," MJ replied, licking her lips, then she seemed to catch herself. "If he weren't such an arrogant jerk," she corrected.

"If you don't mind my saying so, and you probably will because I know this is brash, but maybe you have a type?" Alex said gently.

MJ snapped. "What are you talking about?"

"Well, Dixon wasn't exactly Mr. Congeniality."

"You can say that again," William said.

"No, he wasn't. He was powerful. He knew what he wanted. So does he," MJ said, pointing at Mike, "so yes, maybe I do have a type."

"I knew it!" William said.

MJ lowered her head, shaking it. "Crap."

"Yep. You just gave up the ghost. You and Mike are sittin' in a tree," William taunted. Alex gave him a warning glance that said *don't push it*.

"How old are you, three?" MJ said hotly. "I've heard you going on about your appreciation for beauty. Well, I appreciate strong men. Doesn't mean I have to like them."

"Did you like Dixon?" Alex asked.

"Sometimes. Sometimes I loathed him." MJ stopped. "But not enough to kill him. Especially since I wouldn't be here if it weren't for him. Becca would never have hired me," she spat. "She can't stand me."

"Will that change things? Now that he's gone?"

MJ watched the snake closest to her. "Definitely. Eric promised I'd be the host for the whole series. Said it was all wrapped up and his lawyers made it iron-clad. He told me he did it to spite Becca."

Alex kept her face impassive, but inwardly sighed. It was beginning to seem like the whole show was built around the two half-siblings doing things to spite each other. She thought of the argument in the bar. "I take it that's not the case?"

"No. The bas—sorry, I guess I shouldn't speak ill of the dead, should I? Wouldn't look very good. He changed his mind, he said. Said he wanted to see how well I did with the first episode. Becca's already told me I'm out as soon as we wrap up this show." MJ clutched her arms around her narrow frame, and for the first time, Alex saw tears in her eyes. "What's going to happen to me now?" she whispered.

Across the room, Mike lowered his camera and caught MJ's attention, then tilted his head towards the exit. "C'mon. We're feeding the budgies next."

"Not me," Paul said. "I'm done with this." He pushed his way past everyone and banged the door open. The reptiles turned as one to the sound, and then relaxed.

Chapter 21

MJ pasted a smile on her face as Mike passed her. Mike looked at her and Alex, frowning at MJ. "Buck up, buttercup," he said to the host. "You've got a job to do." He winked at Alex before pushing through the door and walking quickly uphill. Although the transition had been gradual over the last two days, Alex had now completely reassessed her opinion of him. He wasn't the easy-going man she'd thought him to be. There was something darker, just under the surface. With his rugged romance book cover looks and MJ's affinity for bad boys, Alex could see why she'd be attracted to him. She followed closely behind the young woman. "I owe you an apology," Alex said. "I've been so wrapped up in trying to make sure Emily doesn't take the blame that I haven't stopped to consider how you're feeling. Are you doing ok?"

MJ stopped, shocked. "You're the first person to ask me that," she said. "Thank you."

Alex held back from hugging her. While that was Alex's go-to reaction, she didn't think MJ would welcome it. Instead, she gave her a small smile, squeezed her shoulder, and stepped back to walk next to William.

"That was kind of you," he said.

"I'm missing something," Alex shrugged off his comment.

"She seems pretty upset. Were those actual tears?"

"Yes, but I don't think they were for Dixon. She thought she was set when he promised her she'd be the host for the whole season. That little fight we witnessed at the bar? I'm betting that's when he told her she's on a trial basis."

"Oh man. That would give her motive, wouldn't it?"

"Certainly would." Alex stopped, snapping her fingers. "Wait a minute. Mike and Dennis filmed the fire dancers and the band," she said, stopping so abruptly that William stumbled into her.

"Which means there's video of who was on the terrace."

"Exactly. We need to see that video." Alex sped up to catch Mike. She slowed when they neared Stellar, who was leaning casually against a fence made of rough-hewn logs with her arms crossed.

"Please tell Senator Roscoe," Stellar said and Alex realized she was on the phone, "and use these exact words—while I appreciate his desire to impress his donor with the corner table, it is unavailable for the evening in question. However, I would be more than happy to accommodate him with the Kennedy booth. It's spacious and I believe it is, frankly, the best table in the house. Got it? Good. Thank you. Send me a text when it's all confirmed. I appreciate you," Stellar said, then hung up. She shook her head at Alex. "Politicians. They all want the best seat in the house. So we give them what we have and then tell them it's the best seat in the house."

"I suppose when you're dealing with those types, a little white lie doesn't hurt," William said.

"Young man, do not impugn my integrity. I may work and live in Washington, but I don't play their games. Every seat in the house *is* the best seat in the house, because I designed it that way."

William laughed. "Of course you did. Reprimand earned and accepted. And you can scold me any time you want, as long as you continue to call me young."

Stellar winked and began making another call while Alex and William continued uphill.

They turned the corner, and Alex saw the chefs and Mike enter the budgie enclosure. She stopped and bent over, putting her hands on her knees and taking deep breaths. While she'd gradually been getting back into shape, the higher elevation was taking a lot out of her. Because the zoo was on the side of a mountain, getting from one exhibit to another wasn't anything like strolling Lincoln Park Zoo back home. That lovely place was blissfully flat except for a few minor inclines.

"Drink this," William said, handing her his bottle of water.

Alex waved it off. She straightened up and took a swig from her own bottle, draining it. William studied her. "I see a sign for restrooms up there, so there's probably a fountain. Give me your bottle and I'll refill it," he said, holding out his hand.

Alex passed him the bottle, grateful for her friend, yet slightly annoyed at his mothering. "Stop," he said. "I know that look. I'm not babying you. I'm watching out for a friend who's sometimes too independent for her own good. Say thank you."

"Thank you," Alex smiled.

"You're welcome. Now go feed birds."

Alex watched him walk up the hill—everywhere they walked in this zoo was uphill, it seemed—then turned to enter the aviary. She was immediately assaulted with the sound of hundreds of birds chirping and flapping their wings. Budgies, canaries, and parrots flitted from branch to branch, from ceiling beam to window ledge, their songs filling the space. With Paul's issue with animals, she could understand why he wouldn't want to be in there. Alex, however, loved it.

So did Sergio, LuEllen, and Emily. They laughed as gleefully as children. Ranger Karen had given them rods coated with seeds and they held their arms out, luring the brightly colored birds. Pure delight filled Emily's face as a sunshine yellow budgie landed on the stick and began pecking away. Emily grinned at Sergio. In the background, Mike trained his camera on the two chefs.

Alex waited until he lowered his camera and approached him. "I can't wait to see how you pull all this together."

Mike nodded. "It's going to be fantastic. This setting, and the interplay with those four, is reality show magic."

"I have a confession," Alex said. "I've never seen a reality show."

"Not one?"

"Unless you count Great British Baking Show. But other than that, no. They always seem so, so manufactured. It's fascinating to see behind the scenes."

Mike whipped his camera back up to catch LuEllen trying to kiss a parrot. "I need one of these in LuEllen's Shrimp Shack," the chef declared, looking straight to the lens.

"She certainly knows what she's doing," Mike said, then lowered the camera again.

"I have a favor to ask," Alex said.

Mike turned his head to her quickly, then back to the chefs. "Yes?"

"Would it be possible for me to see the footage you shot of the fire dancers and the band on the terrace?"

"Why?" he asked suspiciously. Alex had been planning to be forthright, but his tone made her change tactics.

"I've started working on one of my pieces about this week, specifically about producing a show like this, and I want to confirm my memories. Chemo brain makes things a little fuzzy," she explained, wincing inwardly about using her treatment to get what she wanted.

Mike focused on her, studying her. "You know there's an NDA, right?"

"Of course. I won't be publishing anything until Becca gives the OK. I just figured it would be more helpful to see the raw footage, you know? It'll make things crisper, make them easier to describe."

He didn't say anything for several seconds, then consulted his watch. He smiled, and it was the easy, affable smile that she'd found so endearing when they first met. It was a smile she no longer trusted. "Absolutely. Come to Room 242 when we get back to the resort and you can review it there."

"Oh, I was hoping I could get a copy of it," Alex said. "You know, so I can refer to it as I'm writing."

"Absolutely not. I had to make a copy so I could give Detective Thompson the original, but if I gave you one? I'd be fired faster than you can say Becca. Speaking of which."

"Mike, we're running a little behind," Becca said as she entered the enclosure, ignoring the birds flying around her head. "I've got a tram waiting. Get them all to Primate World and then we need to get up to the memorial." She looked around. "Where's Paul? Why isn't he with these three?"

"He has a thing about animals," Mike said.

"Of course he does," Becca grunted. She looked out the glass wall and Alex followed her gaze. Paul sat in the tram with his arms crossed like a petulant child. Abbot stood over him with his hands on his hips. It looked like the critic was lecturing the chef.

Something about the two of them bothered Alex, besides the fact that they were both jerks. Becca started for the door. "Seems like I need to remind someone about his contractual obligations. See you up there in five minutes. Don't be late," she said, exiting the building.

As the door opened, Abbot's voice carried. "I know," he said. "You can't keep it a secret much longer."

"Is there a problem?" Becca asked.

Abbot turned around, startled. "Problem?" he said slyly, then looked back at Paul. "No, I don't believe there is. Not for much longer, anyway." With that enigmatic statement, he turned and walked up the hill.

The rest of the group piled into the shuttle. Emily sat next to Paul. Alex took the seat behind her in the back row, which faced backwards. She turned around to talk to her friend. Emily stared, her eyes not seeing anything. The joy from feeding the birds had already dissipated. "This sucks," Emily said.

"Not knowing?"

"Yes. The tension. The worry. I feel like Detective Thompson is going to pop up around every corner, dangling handcuffs and waiting to whisk me away to the pokey."

"Pokey?" Paul scoffed. "Now you sound like this one," he said, pointing to William, who sat next to Alex.

"Pokey is definitely a word I'd use," William agreed.

Emily leaned in close to Alex. Their heads bumped as the driver skirted a pothole. "Have you found anything?" she whispered.

"Nothing concrete—yet. I've got a few viable suspects who have way more motive than you."

"I don't have *any* motive," Emily protested, raising her voice enough to cause Sergio to tilt his head.

"Everything okay back there?" Sergio asked.

"We're fine," Alex said, then whispered to Emily. "I know that, and you know that, but Detective Thompson seems to think your argument with Dixon is motive enough."

Emily sighed. "What is he doing that's taking so long?" she wondered. "I'm actually surprised he hasn't shackled me already, considering what a big deal Dixon was."

"No matter how much he wants to, he still has to have enough evidence. I have a feeling his partner is making sure he does things by the book."

"Detective Miller?" Emily said with skepticism.

Alex nodded. "I did a little digging. It seems Detective Thompson has had a few too many cases thrown out in court. Miller's fairly new, but she's got a stellar record. My guess is she was assigned to him to keep him in line."

Emily shook her head. "Once an investigative journalist ..."

"Apparently."

The shuttle eased to a stop and they filed out. Paul hung back. Becca walked over to him; she talked quietly. Paul leaned in. Alex couldn't hear what he said, but whatever it was, it caused the color to drain from Becca's face. She stood motionless, her mouth agape. She squinted at the chef, looked him up and down, then nodded her head ever so slightly. "We'll talk later," she said, loudly enough for Alex to hear. "You, follow me," she said to the group.

William and Alex looked at each other. "Curiouser and curiouser," William said.

"Um hmm," Alex replied. She walked towards the primate enclosure, but kept her eyes on Paul. A realization dawned.

"What? What what what? You have to tell me what you just figured out," William needled.

"Not yet. It's way too crazy. I need to think."

"And investigate," Emily said.

"Yep." Alex stopped, prompting Emily to stop with her. "Do not worry, okay? It's all starting to come together. I should know what happened this afternoon. You're going to win this thing. You'll get your kitchen. And I'm going to find out who did this."

Chapter 22

The group leaving Primate World was uncharacteristically quiet. It was the fourth day of non-stop activity. Throw a murder in the middle and it was no wonder. Alex sat in the back row of the tram. She liked the unobstructed view it provided. She turned around and realized she hadn't seen Stellar or Jo for awhile. Just as they were about to take off, Jo slid into the seat next to her. The two held on as the vehicle jumped forward.

Abbot shouted. "Watch it! I almost fell off."

"Sorry," the driver called. "This thing's a little touchy."

"It's not the only thing that's touchy," Jo said, her head turned.

Alex followed her gaze. Jo was looking at Abbot, who was glaring at Emily. "He's really got it out for her doesn't he?" Alex asked.

"Pay no mind to him," Jo said. "He's harmless. All anger and nothing to back it up."

"I'm not so sure about that," Alex mused. She looked at the stuffed animal Jo held in her lap. "Aw, isn't that adorable?"

"Meet Giles the Giraffe. I adopted him." Jo pulled out her phone and showed Alex the adoption certificate granted by her donation to the zoo. "He's why I missed the budgies and the primates, but we long and lanky types have to stick together."

"You could say you stuck your neck out for him," William quipped from the next row. Sergio groaned.

The shuttle stopped much smoother than it had started. Alex craned her neck to look towards the top of a tall stone tower. Chimes rang out. "That means it's quarter after," a ranger explained, inviting them to follow the path up to the Shrine of the Sun. "Been tolling every fifteen minutes since 1937, when Spencer and Julia Penrose dedicated this memorial for Will Rogers himself."

Behind Alex, Harriet huffed. "More steps. Great."

"You don't have to climb them, you know," Paul said to her, his gentle tone surprising Alex.

"Yes, I do. As you've pointed out so often, it's my job, isn't it? So fine. Let's get this over with." Harriet trudged towards the entrance to the shrine. Paul walked closely behind her. William and Alex looked at each other and shrugged, then followed after them.

"The rooms and staircase aren't terribly large, so you'll want to go a few people at a time," the ranger warned.

After quickly admiring the murals and photographs that lined the walls on the first floor and stairway, Alex decided she'd have to come back to get a better look. There was simply too much to see. At each landing, Alex paused to get her breath. They were now at over 8,000 feet. While she didn't have the fear of heights that Harriet did, she missed the easier views from home. There, if she wanted to see a horizon, she took an elevator.

Her hesitation evaporated the moment she stepped out on the viewing platform near the top of the tower. She and William walked towards the balcony's edge, a stone wall shaped like the top of a rook.

"Is that Kansas?" William said. "I can see Kansas from here. What's that flash of red? Oh yeah—ruby slippers."

Paul, who stood beside Harriet against the tower, spoke up. "You do know there's more to Kansas than Dorothy," he said derisively.

"Just having a little fun," William said. "Harriet, I'm proud of you."

Harriet gulped, grimaced, then quickly walked to the door. She shrieked as Abbot bumped into her. "Watch where you're going," she commanded.

Abbot sneered. He pushed his way past Paul, who was following Harriet, towards the tower viewer. Behind Abbot, Jo floated through the door. Giles the Giraffe's long neck and head looked out from the cross-body bag strapped around Jo's torso. Jo moved towards the corner of the platform and posed with her back to the view, pulling out her phone to take a video.

"Hello, my Jo-lly Rogers," she began. Before she could say another word, Abbot rushed over, grabbed Giles from the bag, and threw the stuffed giraffe over the edge. "What are you, twelve years old?" he sneered. Alex and William gasped. "You beast!" Jo shouted. "You absolute, unmitigated beast! What is wrong with you?" A gloating smile crossed Abbot's face. He looked positively pleased with himself. Jo looked down, searching for the plush toy while filming the action. She straightened and focused on the camera. "My lovelies, this is exactly the type of person you don't want to be. No, no, I'm not going to show you who it was. Suffice it to say that he is obviously one miserable person and nothing you nor I could do is going to change that. We will not let him get to us, deal?"

William pulled out his phone and opened the app. Alex leaned over his shoulder and they watched the comments pour in. "We love you, Jo," they said. "That's right; don't let 'em get to you," etc.

Alex focused on Abbot. His dark expression filled with malev-olence. Jo's outlook was all well and good, but Alex was suddenly afraid for her. "Jo," she said. "Why don't we go down and see if we can find Giles?"

Jo, who'd resumed staring over the edge searching for the stuffed giraffe, straightened to her full height. She strode regally past Abbot, ignoring him even as he walked with her and strained his neck to try to get her attention. He looked ridiculous.

"I did you a favor," he said. "What grown man needs a child's toy? Oh, that's right, you're not a man, are you?"

William placed himself in front of Abbot. "Jo Primrose is a bigger and better person than you will ever be."

Abbot snorted. "Of course *you'd* think that."

Sergio walked through the open door, Emily following closely behind him. The platform was becoming increasingly crowded. Alex moved away from the half-wall, afraid that if the brewing confrontation erupted she'd be thrown over the edge. "I agree with William," Sergio growled, "and that's something I thought I'd never say."

"So do I," Emily said, pushing around Sergio to stand in front of him and pull Jo next to her. Emily put her arm around Jo's narrow waist. Alex moved to Jo's other side and did the same. "As do I," she agreed.

Abbot's eyes darted from one person to the next. The group had clustered near the doorway and faced Abbot. He stood, isolated, his back to the never ending horizon, his hands bunched into fists. One by one, his fingers relaxed. He cleared his throat, then began to retch. "Excuse me," he said, then pushed his way through them, rushing downstairs, his coughing echoing in the tall, narrow stone chamber.

"That's it," Jo said. "You're all officially Jo-lly Rogers, whether you like it or not."

"We certainly shivered his timbers," William said.

Alex patted Jo's back and stepped aside. "Now where were we. Oh, that's right. Shall we go find Giles?"

They exited the building, single-file, and the ranger greeted them, holding the stuffed giraffe. "You found him!" Jo exclaimed, hugging the plush toy to her chest.

"That was all these two," the ranger replied, pointing to Harriet and Paul.

Alex looked from one to the other. Harriet and Paul? She realized William may have been right, that Paul had been rude to Harriet because he liked her, and with Harriet's smiling face, she might even return the affection. Alex shook her head. She'd never understand the dynamics that brought people together.

"Told you," William whispered. "However, I do not see that ending well. Those are two emotionally stunted people if I've ever met them."

"I can hear you," Harriet huffed, then moved away from Paul. "There's nothing to end. We simply searched for Jo's toy. That's it."

"Whatever you say, my dear. Whatever you say."

Alex watched Jo, who'd stepped to the side to shoot another video and show her legions of fans that Giles had been recovered safely. Abbot wasn't anywhere she could see, and Alex assumed he'd gone back to the tram. Becca walked up the path towards them, focused on her phone, as usual. As the producer neared the group, she looked up. "Jo, my deepest apologies. I never should have let Eric talk me into including him. I'll remove him immediately."

"You have nothing to apologize for," Jo said, walking over to place her hand on Becca's shoulder. "And you will not remove him. I deal with people like that every single day of my life. I may look like a frail little flower—"

Becca snorted.

"—but this skin is thicker than a hippo's. I just use way better moisturizer," she winked. Everyone laughed with her and the collective tension dissipated.

"You're a better person than I," Becca said. "C'mon, everyone. It's time to start back. Chefs, you'll have a break of about thirty minutes and then we'll go to the showroom. You'll prep there before we head to the Garden and I want to make sure you've got plenty of time for dinner tonight. Writers, you'll be on your own until five when we meet in the lobby again." She turned to walk down the short path.

LuEllen, who'd been resting on one of the benches while everyone else climbed, approached William and Alex. "Well, that was a whole can of crawdads. First Harriet and Paul come out of the tower, which was a shocker since they were actually being nice to each other, then Abbot comes barreling out looking greener than a gator in a helicopter. Teach me to sit and rest my weary bones. What'd I miss?"

William filled her in, using Jo's TikTok videos to illustrate.

"What a swamp rat. No, that's an insult to swamp rats."

They reached the tram. Abbot sat in the front row and the rest crowded three across into the remaining seats to avoid sitting near him. William patted the thin space of cushion next to him, but Alex thought of the way the tram lurched when it started and decided to sit next to the critic. She sat down, watching him.

"Say it," he said, his eyes focused on his phone.

"Say what?" Alex asked.

He expelled a deep breath. Alex could smell the sour stench of vomit. "*Why are you so mean?*" he mimicked, in a nasal, sing-song voice. "*Why can't you be nice?*' I know your type. You sit there and judge me when you have no idea, none at all."

Alex waited until he looked up and faced her. The rest of the passengers continued to talk, ignoring the two in the front behind the driver. Abbot breathed again and Alex resisted covering her nose, turning away, or grimacing from the stench of his breath. "So?" she asked. "Why are you so mean?"

"Wouldn't you like to know," he snorted. "You'll run to your little friends and you'll write your little blog post all about the big bad mean critic just so you can get some click bait. Don't think for one second you fool me. I know your type. I know all your types." He'd leaned in and was now inches away from her face. The tram swerved and he started to fall into her. He caught himself, then pulled back, glaring at her impassive expression.

Alex reached into her bag and pulled out a breath mint. She handed it to him silently. He took it, looked at the white tablet, breathed directly into her face, then threw the mint away. Alex watched it bounce on the asphalt. She smiled a small, knowing curve of her lips.

The tram stopped in front of the entrance to the zoo and Alex hopped out. William rushed towards her and began patting her all over. "What are you doing, you goof?" she asked.

"Making sure you're all in one piece. That man could cause bodily harm simply by proximity."

"I can hear you," Abbot said.

"Don't care," William called. Stellar sauntered out of the park and joined the group as they headed to the shuttle. "And where have you been, Oh Capital One?" William laughed at his joke.

"Checking out the restaurant set-up, my dear. Getting some ideas." She turned to Becca. "Thanks for setting that up."

"Glad you could connect. Alright, everybody, let's go. We've got a show to finish up."

Chapter 23

Alex sat at the desk in her room reviewing her notes. She'd be meeting Mike to go over the video in a few minutes, and she wanted to make sure everything was fresh in her mind. Satisfied, she stuffed the notebook in her bag and went to collect William. "Thanks for going with me," she said when he opened his door.

"Wouldn't miss it. Besides, any time a man says 'come to my room,' it's good to have back-up. Unless it's me inviting you, of course."

"Of course."

They crossed the lagoon and found Mike's room in the main building. Alex knocked and Mike answered the door, his bare chest glistening with beads of water. Bits of shaving cream dotted his jawline. William reached over Alex's shoulder to wipe one off. "Missed a spot," he said.

Mike stepped back to open the door wide. "I didn't expect you," he said, frowning at William. "Although I guess I should have."

"That's right! Two peas and all. Thanks for the show," William winked.

They entered a spacious suite. A large dining room table was covered with monitors, computers, and other equipment. "This is quite the set-up," Alex commented.

"Becca didn't want to spare any expense for her little project," Mike said. He grabbed a shirt off the couch, put it on, then pulled out a chair in front of one of the larger monitors. "Dixon wasn't too thrilled. Probably thought it took money away from him, but he didn't want to deal with the details, so here we go. Have a seat." Alex sat down and Mike bent over her to reach the mouse. She could smell his shaving cream. Barbasol? Seemed to fit in with his whole flannel-wearing persona.

William sat in a chair next to her, scooting it close, and leaned in as Mike pulled up the footage from the evening Dixon was murdered. He'd queued it to when people began walking outdoors for the night's entertainment. Alex opened her notebook to a blank page. She noted time stamps and names, paying particular attention to when someone appeared, as well as when they walked off-screen.

They watched the video, the scene reflecting much of what she and William had hashed out that morning: the band setting up in the corner, LuEllen and Stellar facing each other, their arms resting on the back of their couch, Alex and William taking a seat in the section closest to the showroom. There was Sergio, sitting with his head leaned back. Emily sat down next to him. The two talked for a moment, and then she got up. That's when Paul approached Sergio and extended his hand. MJ leaned against the wall in the corner next to the door, tapping on her phone. The camera lingered on her; she looked up and smiled seductively into the lens. Dixon suddenly blocked the view, standing in front of the camera with his hands on his hips. He said something, then pointed to the stage and walked towards it.

A blur crossed in front of the lens and Alex saw a flash of pink. "That must have been when Emily went back in."

"Why did she?" William asked.

"Can you pause, please?" Alex asked Mike, keeping her eyes focused on the screen. "It came up during our interview. She had to go to the bathroom, then she wanted to clean up her station and put her ingredients away. She can't abide a dirty kitchen."

"May I?" Mike asked, then restarted the video. The fire dancers filed past onto the terrace. From the angle of his camera, it looked like Mike was walking around the edge of the terrace, capturing the entire outdoor platform. She could see his assistant, Dennis, in the corner of the frame.

"Stop," Alex commanded. She pulled out her phone and took a screenshot.

"Hey, you can't–" Mike objected.

"It's for my use only. I promise."

Mike looked down at her notepad. "I thought you wanted to see this video for your article. You said you wanted to 'refresh your memory' or some such crap. This looks an awful lot like you're trying to figure out who went where and when."

Alex looked up at him innocently. "Of course I am," she said. "It's my training; I have to have all the details right or I get complete writer's block."

Mike frowned again. Alex could tell he didn't buy it, but she smiled and hoped he'd let them finish watching. "And you?" he asked William. "Why do you need to watch this? Do you get writer's block, too?"

William gave him an abashed smile. "I'm a writer, aren't I? Happens to the best of us. I'm here because Alex and I have been talking about collaborating on a piece and covering different aspects. Four eyes, two views, you know."

"No, I don't, but we're almost through. Let's get this over with." Mike restarted the video. The camera zoomed in on the performers, the jazz band blurry behind them, then tightened up on one of the flaming batons. It looked like that was the end of the video until it suddenly whipped towards the showroom, capturing Alex jumping up and running inside and Abbot nearly plowing into her, then bending over. Mike reached over and clicked stop. "I'm sure you don't need any of *that* for your story," he said snidely.

Alex stared at the screen. In the background, Emily stood with her hands covering her face, and Alex could see the soles of a pair of shoes at her feet, the rest of the body hidden by the island. There was a blur on the left of the screen, like someone was running into the hallway. Becca stood in the foreground with a frown on her face.

"Murder in Still Life," William murmured. Alex surreptitiously raised her phone and took another screenshot. Mike pressed a button and the screen went black.

Alex stared at the monitor, chewing on her lower lip, then pushed back from the table and stood. "Thank you, Mike. This has been more helpful than you could know," she said, returning her notebook to her bag and following William to the door. As it closed behind them, she heard the cameraman mumble under his breath.

"That's what I'm afraid of."

Max set two Manhattans on the mahogany bar. The liquid shimmered as he slid the full martini glasses towards Alex and William. They sat in their now customary places at the corner in The Hotel

Bar. William gingerly picked his up, then waited with his drink held in mid-air. "Hello. Earth to Alex."

Alex stared at the image on her phone, using two fingers to enlarge the picture. At William's comment, she blinked and looked up. She reached for her glass, sipped a bit off the top, and then gently touched her rim to his. "Cheers," she said. "Sorry for the sip, but my hands aren't nearly as steady as yours."

"You're forgiven. Now tell me."

"I think I know who that is," she said. She pointed to the blur in the screenshot she'd taken of the showroom from Mike's monitor. It seemed to be someone entering the hallway. Alex looked up as a tall blond sat next to William at the bar. "Hello, MJ. I was just thinking of you."

"Oh really? I didn't think you were that type," she said, then winked at Max as he placed a rocks glass filled with ice and a clear liquid in front of her. Alex noticed she went through the motions of flirting, but she seemed subdued.

"I have to ask you something," Alex said.

MJ sighed heavily. "No, I did not kill Eric Dixon. We've been over this, alright? And I didn't try to poison him either. He was my meal ticket. Do I strike you as stupid?" She laughed wryly. "On second thought, don't answer that."

Alex pointed to the blur in the image on her phone. "Is this you?"

MJ stared at the image and her face closed. "I didn't do it. I didn't kill him."

"I know," Alex said, and William sucked in a quick breath. She glanced at him. "That's what I was getting ready to tell you. I'm pretty sure I know what happened." Alex turned back to MJ. "How long have you known Mike?"

"A few years," MJ said, contradicting what Mike had told them. She waved her hand. "We'd dated, and then I started working for Eric and the shrew, and one thing led to another."

"But you kept in touch?"

"No, actually. Once Eric left his wife for me, I cut all ties. But then Eric told me about this show and I thought of Mike. I felt bad for the way things ended with him, but a girl's gotta do–"

"What a girl's gotta do," William finished. "This explains so much."

"Like what?" MJ asked.

"You know, the not-so-subtle glances in between the bits about how much you dislike each other. Then there was your little confession this morning. Neither of you are very good actors."

MJ laughed ruefully. "Oh, you'd be surprised. I think he's a very good actor. He certainly had me fooled."

"About what?" Mike said softly. They'd been so focused on their conversation they hadn't noticed him walk into the bar. Alex realized this had been happening to her a lot and vowed to be more observant.

"I know, Mike. I know you did it," MJ said, and tears–real tears–pooled and slid down her face.

"Did what? Wait? You think I killed Dixon?" Mike looked genuinely hurt. "MJ, how could you think I'd do that?"

"No, not that. You tried to cover it up. To protect me. But Mike, I didn't kill him. I can't believe you'd think I'm a murderer." She dropped her face in her hands and started sobbing.

Mike sat down next to her and gently smoothed her hair behind her ear. Alex's and William's heads swiveled back and forth between the two.

"Is this what you figured out?" William whispered. MJ and Mike turned to look at him.

Alex sighed. "I love you, dear William, but it's time you gave up any pretense of believing you can whisper. I think you're even louder when you try."

"Doesn't change my question."

"Yes, Alex, please, do tell. Is this what you figured out, and why you really needed to see that video?" Mike asked, leaning forward.

"I figured a lot of things out, and one of the main ones is that you're both idiots," Alex said, frustrated. William gasped. Alex was rarely rude. "You obviously care for each other. However, Mike did think you killed Dixon, or at least tried to."

"But I didn't," MJ sputtered.

"I know that, and you know that, and if you let me finish, Mike will, too, and he'll realize what an idiot he's been, that he completely messed up Detective Thompson's investigation, and because of that, he's put my friend in imminent danger of being arrested for something she emphatically did not do."

The three of them stared at Alex, silenced by her passion.

"MJ, Mike knew this blur was you leaving the showroom. He can barely take his eyes off you, so of course he'd remember where you were. He also knew you didn't stab Dixon, but when news came out about the poisoning, he thought you did it."

MJ snapped her head to Mike. "Is this true? You thought I was trying to poison him? You *do* think I'm capable of murder."

"Anybody who spent any time with that man would be capable of murder," Mike muttered. "You made a lot of his drinks. I thought you were slipping antifreeze in. It would have been understandable."

"Unbelievable," MJ said, wrenching her hands from his.

"If I may continue?" Alex asked. "When news came out about the poisoning, Mike decided to muddy the waters by putting the antifreeze in one of the canisters. Everybody'd heard about Emily's fight with Dixon. It would point the police even more firmly in her direction." Her voice was laced with disgust. "He did it to protect you, and he didn't give a damn who else it hurt."

MJ looked up at Mike. "You did that for me?"

William snorted. "Lady, I wouldn't be getting all googly-eyed. Pinning poison on an innocent person is not a romantic gesture. It's the action of a psychopath."

Alex stood up. "I haven't said anything to the police or to Becca. I suggest you do before I have the opportunity," she looked at her watch, "which will be in about an hour. Max," she said, turning to the bartender, "I'm taking the rest of my drink up to my room." When he nodded, she began walking out. William followed behind her.

"What next, Ms. Poirot?" he asked.

"We get proof of who did it, before it's too late."

"I take it that means you know who?"

Alex nodded. "Yes. Yes, I do."

Chapter 24

William drained his glass and set it on the desk with a thump. "No. Way." He picked up the phone. "I'm going to need another one of these," he said, then tapped the button for room service.

Alex pressed on the lever, hanging up the call. "We don't have time. We have to be in the lobby in twenty minutes, and it takes ten just to get there."

"Fine, but seriously—when did you figure this out?"

"I had a hunch this morning. Paul said something to Becca and she looked shell-shocked. Then it clicked. I needed to get to my computer to confirm my hunch."

"Paul is a Dixon. Who knew?" William said in wonder.

"Apparently nobody, except for him, his mother, and Abbot."

"How did Abbot know?"

Alex used the mousepad to scroll to the top of the newspaper article they'd been reading. The headline read: *Dixon Paternity Suit Settled; Mother Remains Anonymous*. Alex pointed to the byline. "Arnold Abbot's been here his whole life. Before making his name as a food critic, he paid his dues just like every other journalist."

"So Dixon Senior was a randy one."

"It would seem so. Looks like Abbot put the pieces together. He knew about Becca, of course. Dixon had dumped Eric's mother for hers and they got married; that's why she has the name."

"But Paul's mom was just a piece on the side." William peered closer at the monitor, scrolled down, and whistled. "That's quite a hefty settlement. Aha. Paul said his mom invested in *Siren*; that's how he could open a place in ritzy Malibu when he was so young."

Alex opened another tab and typed a quick search. She pulled up an article announcing the restaurant's opening. It was a red carpet gala attended by a who's who of celebrities. The news story detailed how Carly Winston, the restaurateur's mother, had been a prominent philanthropist since arriving in Malibu twenty years earlier from Colorado Springs. She was a statuesque blond wearing a sparkling red dress, and she stood proudly next to a much younger Paul. The similarity to the youthful Dixon she'd seen in photos at the showroom was striking. In this photo, Paul grinned, holding a pair of giant scissors poised to cut a ceremonial ribbon.

"Like father like son," Alex said. She tapped the woman's face. "The Dixons seemed to have a type."

"Is she still alive?" William asked. He picked up his glass to take a sip, then put it back down as he realized it was empty.

Alex typed quickly and found the woman's obituary. "No. She passed away," Alex stopped. She bounced her finger on her lip. "Last year. Right before they began recruiting chefs for the show. What do you want to bet she left behind some information for her son?"

"And that's how he got on the show," William exclaimed. "It's been bugging me. He's good, but the other three seem to be so much more creative. I wondered how he could have been chosen to represent the west, when I know there are better chefs. I thought maybe they just weren't interested. Instead," he continued, "he told his brother–"

"Half-brother."

"–he'd better put him on the show, and he better win, or else he'd be coming for his share of the Dixon pie. Now that's a motive if I've ever heard of one."

"It's all supposition, of course. We can't prove any of it," Alex said, then stood up as the alarm on her phone notified her it was time to go. After nearly missing the train on Pikes Peak, she'd decided to start keeping better track.

"No, but I bet Detective Thompson could, if he'd listen to us," he said, following her into the hallway.

"That's a big *if.* Considering Becca told us Thompson's fixed DUIs for Abbot, I wouldn't be surprised to find out he's crossed even bigger lines. I don't trust him to do what's right. I think we should talk to Detective Miller."

"I thought she didn't like you?"

"I never said that. I just said she's by the book. That's why I think she'll listen. There's no way she'll want to arrest the wrong person."

They walked the rest of the way to the lobby in silence. They were the first to arrive, except for Mike and Becca. Mike stared at the floor while Becca berated him. He looked up and Becca turned to face Alex and William. "I hear I have you two to thank for this." She did not sound grateful. Before Alex could protest, she raised her hand. "Stop. You did the right thing. As did you, Mike, finally. Call Dennis and tell him he needs to take over filming for tonight. He's at the showroom with the chefs, right?" Mike nodded. "Fine. Then I want you to call Detective Miller and tell her what you did. We may, or may not, see you tonight, depending on what she decides to do."

"Detective Miller?" Mike questioned.

Becca scowled. "Was I not clear? Yes, Detective Miller. I do not want you calling that incompetent blowhard Thompson. He'd probably offer to keep it off the books and then send you an invoice."

The rest of the journalists trickled into the lobby, followed by MJ. She walked tall, and when she saw Mike, she gave him a small, sad smile. She stopped briefly next to Becca, then walked out of the hotel and into the waiting shuttle.

Alex boarded last. Abbot sat in his normal spot in the front row and glared at Alex as she walked by, but she ignored him. The ride was subdued. As they drove towards the site for the evening's dinner, she thought about Paul. According to his mother's obituary, she had never married, and there was no mention of a father. Alex wondered what it would have been like to have grown up without a dad, or any sort of father figure, and then to find out in your forties you were related to a name you'd known your entire life. During their interview, Paul had told Alex how his mother insisted they outfit the entire kitchen with Dixon appliances. *Only the best for my son*, she'd said. Reflecting on the conversation, Alex remembered his words had been laced with bitterness. She wondered if he'd even wanted to be a chef, or if his mother had directed that part of his life, too.

They pulled into the parking lot. Alex stood and stretched. It had been such a long week. She was glad tonight was the last dinner. She was ready to be back home in her nice, safe, drama-free Chicago condo. From her spot in the back, Alex watched Abbot as he stepped off the bus. Instead of waiting for the group like a normal person would, he started on his own down a path that curved gently, white jagged slabs towering to his left. He traced his hand along the wooden fence meant to keep people on the path, then snatched it away and sucked on his index finger. *Must have gotten a splinter*, Alex thought. *Couldn't have happened to a nicer person.*

She moved forward with the rest of the judges and writers. Becca led them in the same direction as Abbot. Dormant tiki torches lined the way towards sentinels of red sandstone. They didn't walk far before Alex saw white linen-topped tables showcasing extravagant floral centerpieces. Heat lamps flickered every few yards. Makeshift chefs' stations had been set up to one side of a stone outcropping that formed the center of a plaza. On the other side, hidden so they couldn't see the chefs, were three bistro tables. Jo and Stellar stood among them, holding drinks and talking. Abbot walked away from the other judges and disappeared behind the outcropping. *He's going to cheat and try to see what the chefs are making. The little sneak*, Alex thought. Servers milled about, adding place settings to the tables. A pair of bars flanked the seating area. A table set up behind each bar contained rows of wine, top shelf liquor, and bins filled with ice. This was going to be one heck of a closing dinner.

William by her side, Alex stopped to take it all in. They stood silently, watching as Paul deftly used a small knife to extract seeds from a pomegranate. He looked up and smiled at Harriet. Alex hoped for the other woman's sake that her hunch was wrong. She knew who she wanted to be the murderer, but she'd been caught by her dislike of someone before and this time she needed to be sure. Paul had the biggest motive of anyone, besides Becca. What did it say about Dixon that the two most likely people to kill him were related to him?

Alex made her way towards Emily. All four chefs were completely focused on their tasks, ensuring their prep would be done before the final competitive dinner. Important guests, including the mayor, would begin arriving shortly. Becca had timed it to coincide with the setting sun. Dennis walked from one station to the other, shifting the camera to focus alternatively on the chefs and what they were preparing. It seemed like Mike's absence didn't affect him and he had it under control.

Alex neared Emily's station. Abbot hovered in the background, hugging the outcropping and trying to avoid the camera. Alex poised to warn Emily about the critic when her friend looked up from her dicing and smiled. The pleased look slipped as Emily's gaze shifted. She focused beyond Alex and froze, her knife suspended. Alex turned and her throat clenched as she watched Detectives Thompson and Miller stride purposefully up the path, both flexing their hands. Uniformed officers formed a human barricade behind the detectives, turning away any oncoming pedestrians.

Becca walked towards Thompson and Miller. "Well, this is a surprise. We weren't expecting police protection for our little shindig," she said. "I'll be sure to thank Mayor Ingram when she arrives."

The detectives continued walking towards the chefs' stations. They stopped within feet of Alex. Miller glanced at Thompson, who spread his feet and crossed his arms over his chest. They were close enough to Alex she could see a yellow stain on the collar of the detective's white button-down shirt.

"Ms. Dixon, please don't make this harder than it needs to be," Thompson said.

"You have to stop this," William gasped in Alex's ear.

Alex held up her hand to quiet him. "Wait," she said. "Maybe they're not here for Emily."

William looked at her, dumbfounded. "I know you're an optimist, but you have to see he's going to arrest her. He's looking right at her!"

Alex knew he was right, but she couldn't believe her best friend, the woman who'd comforted her, commiserated with her, lifted her up, made her laugh, could be arrested for murder. It simply wasn't possible. She held her breath and stared at the detectives, willing them to arrest Paul instead.

Thompson glared at William, then turned back to face Becca. He opened his mouth to speak, but stopped when he noticed Miller walking away from him towards the chefs. Miller unsnapped her holster and slowly pulled out her gun. "Sir, please put the knife down and step away from Ms. Kincaid."

Alex spun her head back towards the chefs, expecting to see Paul threatening Emily, but he stood frozen at his station. His eyes focused on the tableaux next to him. Alex gasped. Abbot half-hid behind Emily, one arm wrapped around her waist, the other holding a knife against her throat. Abbot gripped the black handle so tightly all color had vanished from his knuckles. Emily gulped, the motion startling Abbot. He pressed the knife closer; a trickle of blood dripped down her chest. Sergio started towards them, clutching his own knife.

"Back off," Abbot shrieked, pulling Emily tighter to him. She tried to turn her head to Sergio, the look on her face pleading with him to listen to Abbot.

Sergio raised his hands and stepped back a few feet, then placed his knife back on his station. "OK, man, OK. Look, just let her go. She doesn't deserve this."

"Ha!" Abbot barked. "She doesn't deserve this? She deserves anything I choose to do to her. The way she treated me, the way you've all treated me. So high and mighty. Just like Dixon, the backstabbing cheat. He got what he deserved."

"Mr. Abbot..." Becca began.

"Don't you start with me. You're worse than he is. Now step back. All of you. I'm going to take Ms. Kincaid here and you're not going to follow. You do; she dies. It's that simple." Filled with self-righteousness, Abbot seemed to stabilize, and Alex was truly terrified. Fear grasped her. Her heart rate exploded. She could feel the blade against her own throat, as surely as if Abbot were threatening her instead of her best friend. Alex swallowed carefully, afraid if she moved, even minutely, it would startle Abbot and the knife would slip and Emily would be gone. He squeezed Emily tighter around the waist, practically lifting her, even though she was taller. He had to reach up to hold the knife to Emily's neck, so dangerously close to her carotid artery.

Emily focused on Alex, who straightened her shoulders and returned the direct gaze. *You're going to be OK*, Alex tried to communicate to her. Emily winked. Alex inhaled sharply. *She winked?* Alex thought, incredulously. A man, a crazed man who'd already murdered one person, held a knife to Emily's throat and she winked? Alex took a deep, calming breath, knowing she had to keep a brave face, even though she was terrified for her friend, and even more terrified about what Emily was going to do. That wink meant the impetuous, driven woman was going to do something stupid, Alex just knew it.

"Please," Emily pleaded. "I'm so sorry for anything I've ever done to wrong you." She swallowed, and another drop of blood slid down her throat. With that swallow, Alex could feel her desperation. "You're right," Emily continued. "I don't deserve to be here. I don't deserve to be on any cooking show. I don't even deserve to wear an apron."

Abbot smiled, a wicked, gloating grimace. Spots of color appeared on his knuckles and the knife lowered slightly, ever so slightly; from the relieved look on Emily's face, Alex knew he'd loosened his grip. Emily winked at Alex again. Before Alex could warn her friend to stop whatever fool thing she had in mind, Emily grabbed Abbot's wrist and pulled it away from her neck. She put her thumb on the tender flesh below his hand and pinched his nerves until he dropped the knife, then she stomped on his foot, jabbed an elbow in his gut, and then for her finale, she turned around and kneed him. Abbot doubled over. Emily jumped back as he started to retch. Detective Miller grabbed Abbot's wrists, pulling them behind his back and snapping cuffs on him. The senior detective finally moved, walking towards the shackled man who was still bent over. Thompson stood in front of him and began to read him his rights when Abbot vomited all over the detective's patent leather shoes.

Thompson walked away to clean them off, shaking bits of detritus as he went. Emily strode towards Abbot, pulled back her fist, and punched him, knocking him out of Miller's grasp and onto the ground. She looked down at him and spat, then grabbed a towel off her station, walked to the bar, scooped a handful of ice into the rag, and wrapped it around her fist. She looked up and grinned.

"Classic Emily," Alex said.

"I think I'm in love," said Sergio.

Chapter 25

Abbot sat on the paved path, his hands cuffed behind him. "Arrest her!" he shouted. "That's assault. I'm pressing charges."

Detective Miller looked directly at her partner. "I didn't see anything. Did you?"

Thompson returned her glare, then motioned to one of the uniformed officers to come collect Abbot. "I saw a man threaten a woman with a knife. A man who drew blood. That's what I saw." Thompson bent over the shackled man. "I guess you can do my job for me. I was coming for her, you idiot."

"It was her!" Abbot shouted. "She killed Dixon. Arrest her! Don't forget," Abbot hissed. "I know your secrets."

The detective stared at his feet, then looked at the critic. "Yes, you do, and because of that, I almost got an innocent woman killed."

"I'm not so sure I'd call her innocent," Sergio said, then laughed when Emily elbowed him. "Nice right hook, by the way."

"See?!" Abbot shrieked. "He's a witness. I'm pressing charges," he repeated, even while the officer dragged him away.

"Good luck with that," William called, then bounded over to Emily and kissed her on both cheeks. "You're as fiery as your hair. When you two get married, you need to adopt me."

Emily and Sergio glanced at each other and burst out laughing. Alex walked up to her friend, waiting until she had her attention. She put her hands on her hips. "If you ever take a chance like that again..." Alex scolded.

Emily grabbed her, squeezing her in a tight hug. When she finally released Alex, Emily took her hands. "I'm here. I'm okay."

Alex shook her head. "That was so stupid. He could have killed you."

"But he didn't. You know me. There's no way I'm going to let a weasel do something like kill me."

"Sometimes it's not up to you."

"This time it was. But fine, I promise if a crazed lunatic ever has a knife pressed to my throat again that I will not do anything stupid."

Alex narrowed her eyes. The chances of Emily being in a similar situation were slim to none, but she noticed her friend had created a loophole, because she knew Emily didn't think she'd done anything stupid this time. Alex breathed deeply, and tears fell down her cheeks. "I am so very sorry," she said.

"For what?" Emily asked, still holding her hands.

"I knew Abbot had killed Dixon, but I didn't trust myself because I disliked him so much. I was afraid I was blinded. And then I learned about Paul being a Dixon."

"A what?" Emily sputtered. "Paul is a what?"

Paul walked up, his hands shoved into his pants pockets. "A Dixon. I know, I know. Hard to believe, isn't it?"

Emily analyzed his face. "No. I see it now. But wow. So what's the deal; were you a ringer the whole time?"

"Was this whole dog and pony show rigged?" LuEllen demanded. "I swear I'll skin you like a—"

"Can we keep the knife use to plants and already dead animals, please?" Becca interrupted. "To answer your questions: no, I did not know, and no, the show was not rigged. Paul may have coerced Eric into getting him on the show, but I think you'll all agree he's held his own this week."

"So who poisoned Dixon?" Harriet asked. "And why did Abbot stab him in the back?"

"Poetic justice," Alex answered. She shook her head. "I had all the pieces, but didn't put them together until it was almost too late. Dixon had promised MJ she'd be the host for the entire series, then told her she was a fool to believe that."

"So she poisoned him?" Harriet asked.

"No, that was Abbot. I saw him leaving the storeroom that first night after everybody was gone, but it didn't hit me that he was the one spiking Dixon's vodka."

"But Mike thought it was MJ, so he tried to protect her by putting the antifreeze in one of the canisters," William explained.

"Framing me. Lovely," Emily said.

"I'm guessing Dixon told Abbot he'd be the critic for the entire series, but once he had him committed for this show, he told him he'd only be doing the one," Alex said.

"That's exactly what happened," Becca said. "Abbot came to me screaming about Dixon stabbing him in the back." She smacked her forehead. "I can't believe I didn't see it."

"So, Becca," Emily said, uncharacteristically shy. "What happens now?"

Becca grinned. "Have I got a surprise for you. You four, I want to you to act like normal tonight, OK? We've got some heavy-hitters coming and we need to impress them."

"Paul, too? How is that fair?" LuEllen protested, and Emily and Sergio grunted agreement.

"Trust me. Please. I promise you everything's going to be fine. Now, if you'll excuse me, I need to go talk to our remaining judges and then greet the mayor." Becca walked off and left the group standing. They all turned to Paul.

"Beats me," he said.

A server cleared the table and Alex wrapped her pashmina tighter around her shoulders to ward off the chill now that the sun had set. She turned to Harriet, who'd barely taken her eyes off Paul during the entire dinner. It had been another delicious meal. MJ, looking beautiful in a periwinkle evening gown that draped her body like satin sheets, introduced each course with grace. Stellar and Jo gave up any pretense of judging and joined the mayor at her table. A collection of the top restaurateurs in Colorado Springs, and even a few from Denver, had taken a busy Saturday night off to be part of this unique experience in a stunning location. Becca had invited each of them personally, and since they'd either known her from her days growing up in the area or were current customers, they all said yes.

The dinner had been a complete success, except now that it was over, Alex could see the anxiety begin to form in Emily's eyes. Her friend finished cleaning her station and came over to Alex's table, sitting in the empty chair next to William. Sergio and LuEllen stood behind her. Paul stayed at his station.

Becca stood in front of the towering red monolith that formed the center of the plaza. She asked MJ for the wireless microphone and cleared her throat before speaking. "Dennis? Please make sure you get all of this."

She waited for the cameraman to focus on her, then cleared her throat again.

"Is she nervous?" William whispered. "I don't think I've ever seen her nervous."

"I can hear you," Becca said, and the table of journalists and chefs laughed. The producer looked at the gathered diners. "When I first came up with the idea for *Dining + Destinations*, I thought it would not only be a good vehicle to promote Dixon Kitchens, but also a way to showcase chefs who might not get the recognition they deserve, or who might need a bit of a hand. I certainly never expected a week like this." She paused for the nervous laughter. "Eric and I may not have seen eye-to-eye, but he was still my brother–half-brother." The laughter increased. Everyone, it seemed, had heard her make the correction over the years.

"Imagine my surprise to learn that I have another half-brother. Paul, can you come here?"

Paul looked up in shock and the crowd gasped. He slowly made his way towards his half-sister and stood awkwardly as she continued. "With Eric gone, one of the judges the culprit–allegedly," she winked, "and one of the chefs a member of the family that's hosting the competition, there is no way we can operate as planned. My apologies, chefs, but one of you is not getting a whole kitchen."

Emily's eyes dropped. Alex reached across and took her hand. Her friend's nails bit into her palm, but she kept squeezing.

"All of you are."

Complete silence covered the plaza. Emily whipped her head up, grinned, then leapt out of her chair and ran towards Becca, tackling her with an enthusiastic hug and nearly knocking the much taller and sturdier woman over. Becca recovered, then spoke into the microphone. "Sergio, LuEllen, can you please join me up here as well? Sergio, in addition to your new appliances, Dixon Kitchens will help you set up that non-profit you've been planning. You know, the one to teach troubled teens how to cook?"

The tattooed man stared at Becca, and Alex swore she saw him wipe a tear.

"LuEllen, how would you like to open your next LuEllen's Shrimp Shack? If you'll have us, we'd like to start planning your Gulf Coast domination."

LuEllen reached up with both hands and planted a kiss straight on Becca's mouth.

"And Emily, in addition to completely outfitting a new space for *Elements*, we'd like to help out with your chef-farmers co-op. Would that be ok?" Emily grinned and gave her a thumbs up.

"What about Paul?" William wondered. "He looks so confused up there."

"Wouldn't you be?" Harriet snapped.

William reached across the table and patted her hand. "Of course I would."

Becca turned to her half-brother. "Paul, can I ask you something, and will you promise to answer me honestly?" He nodded. "Do you enjoy cooking?"

Paul's shoulders dropped. "What kind of question is that?" Harriet muttered.

"Give them a chance," Alex said. "I think I know what she's doing."

"No," he finally answered. "In fact, I hate it."

The crowd gasped. Becca nodded. "That's what I thought. How would you feel about working with me on this show? You would travel the world and find new destinations and amazing chefs, chefs like these three. You are a Dixon, after all."

Paul stared at her, dumbfounded. "Seriously?" he whispered.

"That's how you whisper," Alex said to William.

Becca nodded. Paul swallowed. "I think I'd feel just fine about that."

Epilogue

Candlelight glinted off the knife's edge as the tattooed man slivered a leek. A woman wearing a black apron and sporting fuchsia hair pressed the button on a stopwatch. "Three seconds!" she shouted. "It's a new record." The tattooed man raised both hands in the air, dropped them into a deep bow, and the restaurant erupted in applause. He picked up the blade by its dull side and presented the pink-handled implement to the woman.

"And that, my friends, is Sergio," Emily said. "I hope you enjoy your potato leek soup."

Emily wove through the dining room, stopping occasionally to speak to patrons. The new *Elements* was packed, just as Alex had known it would be. Becca had taken no time at all to follow through on her promises; by the time Emily was back in Chicago, a schematic detailing the appliances she'd receive, as well as plans for expanding her restaurant into the neighboring space were waiting for her. Sergio and LuEllen had similar stories.

William leaned into the man sitting next to him. "See what I mean?" he said, pointing to Sergio. "This just proves how much I love you."

"That, and he's only got eyes for her," the Tom Selleck lookalike said, pointing to Emily. Billy turned to Alex. "I must say, you look wonderful. I can't believe you had surgery yesterday."

She shrugged. "It was minor."

"But it was HUGE!" William shouted. "No more port! No more port!"

"Did I hear somebody call for port?" Emily said, smiling, as she approached their table. The restaurateur nodded, and a server appeared at the table with a tray full of sipping glasses filled with a deep red liquid. "A round of port for the woman who no longer needs one."

Alex picked up her glass and smiled at her friends. The day before she'd had surgery to remove the port her nurses used to inject chemotherapy into her body. Because she was six months cancer-free, it could finally be removed. William had picked up Billy in Door County, and Sergio had come all the way from North Carolina to help her celebrate.

She sipped on the rich, ruby liquid and closed her eyes. This was what mattered. Friendships. Passion. Purpose. She heard Paul was flourishing. No longer trying to live someone else's dream, he'd found his place. Becca had completely restored the reputation of Dixon Kitchens as she used their vast wealth to invest in projects like Sergio's non-profit and Emily's co-op. Abbot had been denied bail after forensics finished analyzing the towel he'd used to wipe his fingerprints from Emily's knife, and subsequently thrown away in the back storeroom. Even Thompson had decided to retire early and Miller had been promoted, and rightfully so.

Alex thought of LuEllen. She'd be seeing her in a couple months to celebrate the opening of her second place. The woman still scared her a bit; she was definitely a force to be reckoned with.

But as she looked around the room, at Emily, who'd been with her during the hardest time of her life *and* punched out a murderer; at William, who kept her laughing; at Sergio, who'd become the brother she'd never had; Alex knew she was surrounded by forces.

And Alex knew that no matter what happened, these forces would always be by her side.

I hope you enjoyed spending time with Alex, William, Emily, and the entire cast. This adventure may be over, but Alex never stays home for long. Her next destination: the sparkling beaches of Gulf Shores, Alabama.

For even more Alex, find out how her travel writing career began—with a crime, of course! She's barely off the plane for her first research trip when she encounters the police. Will the Sonoran Desert, and her new career, prove too hot for her to handle? Visit thelocaltourist.com/go/stolen/ to get your free short story, *Stolen on the Salt River*.

Recipe

Blackened Trout with Cantaloupe Salsa

W ant to recreate Emily's winning dish from the first night of *Dining + Destinations*?

You can use any whitefish if trout isn't available. I've made it with flounder and catfish and both were delicious. You can also pan fry, air fry, or grill the fish. Just don't microwave it. Eww.

Blackened Spice

- 1 1/2 tbsp cumin (adjust to taste)

- 1 1/2 tbsp chili powder

- 1/2 tbsp paprika

- 2 tsp onion powder

- 2 tsp garlic powder

- 1/2 tsp dried oregano

- 1/2 tsp sea salt (adjust to taste)

- 1/4 tsp ground black pepper

Combine.

Cantelope Salsa

- 3 cups diced cantelope

- 1/3 cup diced red onion*

- 1 tbsp honey

- 2 tbsp white balsamic vinegar

- 1/8 tsp ground black pepper

- 1/4 tsp sea salt

- 1/2 tbsp olive oil (make it the good stuff)

- 2 tbsp basil chiffonade

Combine and let chill while the fish cooks.
*If you soak the red onion in water, it takes away some of the sharpness.

Blackened Fish

- 4 filets mild whitefish of choice

- Blackened seasoning

- Olive oil

Preheat oven to 425 degrees. Line a baking pan with aluminum foil or a silicone mat.
Pat the fish with paper towels to dry.

Brush the fish with olive oil, then generously coat with blackened seasoning. Press to make sure the seasoning sticks to the fish. Turn over and repeat.

Bake for 10-15 minutes, depending on thickness of fish.

Serve on a lovely plate and drape with cantaloupe salsa. Add more basil chiffonade if desired.

Eat!

Author Note

One of the coolest things about writing fiction is that I can make stuff up. Granted, it has to make sense (within the world and parameters I also create), but I don't have to be entirely factual. The researcher in me balks at this, but my creative brain tells her to hush; we've got a story to tell.

Revenge in the Rockies takes place in several locations that actually exist. There's the very real city of Colorado Springs. There are also The Broadmoor, Garden of the Gods, Pikes Peak, etc. Pretty much the only location that isn't real is Dixon Kitchens. However, I've adjusted these very real places to suit my needs. There's no zipline at Royal Gorge, although there is a giant swing, which would also terrify the pants off of Harriet. My descriptions of The Broadmoor may or may not accurately reflect this historic resort. (I pulled the room numbers out of my head, so don't go looking for them.) The description of the cog railway is accurate, and if you want to learn more about it and about Seven Falls, head to The Local Tourist. And oh—those stairs to the top of the falls? They're perfectly safe. I know. I've climbed them. Same with Shrine of the Sun.

I mentioned in the Author Note for *Peril on the Peninsula* that, while Alex and I have had similar experiences, she's definitely got a mind of her own. She does and says things I would never do or say. She's definitely bolder. I got to know her even better this time, and I'm looking forward to what she shows me in the next book. And the next one, and the next one...

Acknowledgments

I've often thought writing acknowledgments was hard. Now I realize they're the best part. Not only do they mean the book is done and ready to be in the world, they're also where I can thank—acknowledge, if you will—that I don't do this alone.

There's a reason I call Jim, my husband, my rock, a saint (and why so many other people do, too). I've read stories of authors whose partners aren't supportive, or who tell them to do something else, or who do nothing to make their writing life easier. Jim is the antithesis of those. I have the space I need and the support I crave to follow my passion. I love you, Mr. Goodrich.

My parents. Wow. Multiple phone calls to discuss edits, some of them lasting two hours. They don't hold back. If Mom and Dad see something that doesn't work, is grammatically incorrect, doesn't make sense, or leaves them feeling flat, they tell me. And I love them even more for their honesty. I don't want platitudes; they don't give them. Mom and Dad, thank you for making me a better storyteller. Thank you for believing in me. I love you!

I asked Heidi Kohz if she would read Revenge while I was writing it. I wanted her to simply read it for story and flow. Does it make sense? Does the plot work? Do the characters feel real? But Heidi doesn't do anything halfway. She fixed stuff. She left little comments of joy, like "I love William almost as much as I love Alex." (Me, too.) She helped clean it up and give me the confidence boost I needed. I love you, soul sister!

And Tatiana Abramova. If you need an editor, HIRE THIS WOMAN. Since 2017, she's taken my words and made them better. She improves my wording, my punctuation, my grammar. I've said it before and I'll say it again, and again, and again: she makes me a better writer. I hear her voice in my head: "Too many pronouns." "A comma, I think." "Awkward." With each book, I receive fewer comments, because with each book, I get better. This time, she said something that's now a daily mantra. She told me that I am "an excellent and captivating writer" and "a joy to edit."

Music, Tati, music to my ears. I love you, my friend!

I also want to thank Krista Heinicke at The Broadmoor, PK McPherson with Pikes Peak Attractions, Alexea Veneracion from Visit Colorado Springs, and Laura Cocivera of Percepture. I contacted you as The Local Tourist, with no plans to write a novel based in your area, but here we are. I hope you enjoy this fictional portrayal of your wonderful region.

Finally, thank you to my readers and supporters, with special shoutouts to Lori Helke, Karen Gill, Shelly Harms, Larry and Carol Pratt, Mary Eileen, Henri Goudsmit, Kerrie Kuiper. I hope you enjoy reading this as much as I enjoyed writing it.

Wait'll you read the next one.

Theresa L. Carter

About Theresa L. Carter

Theresa L. Carter is Theresa L. Goodrich's pen name. It's also her maiden name, the name she had when she dreamed at a tender young age (as most authors do) of writing a novel. Theresa is a travel writer and breast cancer survivor. In her debut novel, she took the "write what you know" maxim to heart and created Alex Paige, although she's quick to argue that Alex is definitely her own person.

When Theresa's not traveling, writing, or dreaming about traveling and writing, she likes to cook, read, and decide which bright shiny object she's going to assiduously ignore next.

You can find Theresa on social media @thelocaltourist and at TheLocalTourist.com.

Made in the USA
Monee, IL
06 April 2023